When her marriage to Sacha Kimberly
broke up, Katie had thought Hawaii was
far enough for her to run away from
him—and to conceal the fact that she had
had his child. Now, after five years, Sacha
had caught up with her. And if she didn't
agree to his suggestion he was going to
take the child away from her . . .

SHADOWED REUNION

BY

LILLIAN CHEATHAM

MILLS & BOON LIMITED
15–16 BROOK'S MEWS
LONDON W1A 1DR

First published 1981
Australian copyright 1981
Philippine copyright 1981
This edition 1981

© Lillian Cheatham 1981

ISBN 0 263 73575 3

Set in Monophoto Baskerville 10 on 11½ pt.

Made and printed in Great Britain by
Richard Clay (The Chaucer Press) Ltd,
Bungay, Suffolk

CHAPTER ONE

KATIE LOCKWOOD was stacking old newspapers to be used in packing glassware in her little shop when she saw the name out of the corner of her eye. For a dizzy moment her heart stopped beating, then she took a long, deep breath and licked lips suddenly gone dry. She and Sacha had been parted for almost five years, and it took no more than that—the sight of his name—to send her into a spiral of panic. Feverishly she pulled the paper to her and flattened it out, her eyes seeking the bold black headliner for the two-column article in the centre of the page: 'Sacha Kimberly, renowned artist, in local showing.' Beneath it was a picture, a publicity photo, that showed a dark, saturnine face wearing a slight scowl as he gazed aloofly at the camera.

Katie's hands were trembling as she folded the page. 'Julian Fine, curator of the Fine Galleries, announced today that he had obtained permission to exhibit a series of Kimberly paintings for the month of April.' And today was near the end of April—the twenty-ninth! How had she missed seeing something about this before now? Her eyes skimmed over the rest of the article. 'Mr Fine feels that Honolulu is fortunate to be granted this unprecedented glimpse of Kimberly paintings, a comprehensive group on loan from private collectors as well as from the artist himself. Mr Kimberly, although only thirty-four years of age, is one of the new young artists gaining a reputation both in the United States and abroad. His paintings are in great demand in European capitals and have an immediate market at home.' And then a little biographical note had been added: 'The artist is the son of Paul Kimberly and

5

Mrs Marjorie Tillotson, the sugar heiress. At one time his face was familiar among the younger members of the jet set, but in recent years, he has abandoned his playboy image to devote his time to painting.'

The reporter went on briskly to add that 'The collection, which is insured for one million dollars, includes the famous *Dreaming*, for which Mr Kimberly won the international Llewellyn Memorial Prize.'

Katie was shaking as she searched through the newspapers for the issue dated April the first and found at last what she was seeking. Fearfully she searched for any hint that Sacha was expected to accompany his paintings to the showing, but it was more or less a repeat of the former article, with a few more quotes from Julian Fine and one small, significant addition: 'When asked how Honolulu came to be so favoured, Mr Fine said that the credit must be given to Mrs Clair Wetherell, a close personal friend of Mr Kimberly's. Mrs Wetherell has been active in cultural affairs since returning to her native Hawaii after several years on the mainland. She may be remembered as the former Claire Thorpe.'

Katie sank to a chair and pushed the papers aside dazedly. How Sacha would hate that gushing blurb if he read it—informing the world that his mother was an heiress and he was an ex-playboy! He never referred to his mother, but Katie had gathered that she was a spoiled, pampered society woman, eagerly seeking her pleasures in the so-called 'fun' spots of the world, and only remembering her son when she was between husbands and feeling sorry for herself. And Katie had never heard him mention his father either, although she had been Sacha's wife for almost a year.

She wondered about Claire Wetherell, who was a 'close personal friend'. Was that a hint that she was something more—the latest in a long line of 'close friends', travelling companions, or whatever they called mistresses nowadays? Katie's hand spasmodically clutched the newspaper, and the pain that sometimes tore at her when she remembered Sacha became an acute ache. Unwillingly she recalled Claire Wetherell, whom she had seen on one memorable occasion. The silk patchwork skirt that she had made for sale in the shop, at two hundred and fifty dollars, had been a little steep and she had not expected to get her price right away. But it had sold the very first day to a gorgeous, dark-eyed brunette, a model-type beauty whose exotic looks had been made for its strong, vivid colours. She had paid by cheque and automatically her name had gone on Katie's mailing list: Claire Wetherell.

Carefully Katie tore out the picture and put it on the table. As she moved about the kitchen making her breakfast, her eyes turned again to the dark face, the cynical, all-knowing eyes. Her thoughts were chaotic, churning mostly around the coincidence of Sacha's paintings turning up here in Hawaii—an ocean away from San Francisco, which had been their home while they were married. Apparently it was all due to Claire Wetherell. At their one meeting, Katie had assumed that she was a *haole* like herself, a newcomer to the islands. But apparently she was a native Hawaiian and well known to the moneyed society. Katie wondered if Claire was still married, divorced or what. In spite of having lived in Honolulu for five years, she knew next to nothing about the people who frequented the society pages of the newspapers, and although she might make enquires, she didn't want any hint to float back to Claire Wetherell of her interest. There was a possibility that Sacha might visit her here—might even now be visiting her. Katie's heart lurched at the thought, then quieted. She was not likely to meet him. She couldn't afford to, she reminded herself painfully. He had probably already forgotten her anyway, his marriage a bad memory of misunderstandings and turmoil.

'Mommy, is it Wednesday?'

A small, dark-haired boy stood in the doorway, rubbing his eyes. He was accompanied by a small white dog with a curly tail, who left him to investigate the contents of a food bowl under the sink. Katie held out her arms, and with a chuckle, the child ran into them. His little body was still warm from his bed and he smelled faintly of baby powder, an odour that clung to his blue cotton pyjamas.

Katie hugged him tightly, and he looked up, laughing. She caught her breath at the resemblance to the face that was even now staring at her from the newspaper clipping on the table. Could anyone else see it? It was obvious to her—black eyes and hair and the slim, coltish look that meant that, even at the age of four, Kim was going to be a tall man like his father. He didn't get that look from her, for she was of average height with a deep bosom and full hips that gave her a voluptuous look in spite of her slimness. It contrasted oddly with the demure wholesome face. What had Sacha called her? His Passionate Puritan. With a deliberate effort Katie tore her mind away from painful memories of Sacha and concentrated on her son.

'Yes, it's Wednesday.' She knew what that query meant and a dimple appeared briefly at the corner of her mouth. 'And we're going to do something special. How does a picnic grab you, young man?'

'Sammy too?'

'Sammy too—and Trisha, of course.'

With a sigh of pure bliss the little boy leaned against her for an extra hug before climbing to the table to eat his breakfast. As he tackled his eggs and toast, Katie sat opposite him and sipped her cooling coffee. This was one of her favourite times of the day, when she was granted a few minutes alone with her son before opening the shop. Her eyes warmed with tenderness as she watched him feeding

Sammy bits of egg-soaked bread. He was such a dear, and so good and patient about accepting that she had to put the shop first. From babyhood he had had to take second place to her necessity to earn a living for the two of them. Her eyes roamed over the small serious face wearing a milk moustache. He looked so much like Sacha. One look at the two of them together and it would be obvious to anyone. The only feature he shared with her was his mouth, which was tender and vulnerable with generous, well-shaped lips. It was her best feature, along with her wide-spaced grey eyes that faithfully reflected every mood and changed colour with every emotion. Shadowed by thick, gold-tipped lashes beneath finely arched brows, they were the calm grey of a lake on a summer day right now, as she watched her son. She had a wholesome, outdoors look—a golden girl who spent long hours on Hawaiian beaches under the Hawaiian sun. It was a deceptive look, for Katie seldom had time to spend idle hours on the beaches.

Reluctantly she finished her coffee and cleaned the kitchen, sponging off the counter and table top before starting on peanut butter sandwiches. Along with drinks that she could buy at the beach and a couple of dog biscuits for Sammy, that would be their picnic. She sent Kim and Sammy outside to play, then opened the shop door, but before she did, she carefully put away Sacha's picture between the folds of lingerie in her drawer. Then she returned to the shop and unlocked the door and raised the shades to show they were open for business.

The shop was her pride and joy, her independence. Five years ago, when she had arrived in Hawaii on Aunt Anna's doorstep, scared and pregnant, she had badly needed something to pull her together and restore her slipping confidence in herself. At the time she had not known that her aunt was dying. Aunt Anna kept her secret well until her illness became obvious even to Katie's inexperienced eyes. By then, however, Aunt Anna had a plan—a plan to help her keep her baby. She had suggested opening a shop in the front two rooms of the dingy little bungalow, and before Katie could voice an objection 'Katie's Place' was begun. Aunt Anna lived just long enough to know that she had been right.

After Aunt Anna's death, the baby and the shop had been Katie's salvation. It wasn't good, raising a baby under these circumstances, but at least it had the advantage of being able to keep Kim nearby so that when he cried or needed her, she was right there. Later, when he was older, she had fenced in the small back yard, overshadowed by the towering buildings on either side, and it was here that Kim played with his swing and sandbox.

At noon Katie's neighbour, a bouncing blonde divorcee with a single child like herself, came over to work in the shop. Wednesday was early closing day and Katie usually spent half of it with her son. She was fortunate that Pat Merritt was willing to work whenever she needed her, and in return, Katie included Pat's five-year-old Trisha in whatever plans she had made for Kim.

Pat lived next door in one of the towering high-rise apartments that looked down upon her little house. They had clicked immediately when Pat came into the shop one day, and stayed on for coffee and conversation. Katie, lonely and starved for an adult to talk to, had taken to her at once. Pat had confessed that she was frequently bored and idle, and Katie had offered her a part-time job on the spot. Since then Pat had roped her in on some of the active social life that went on in the apartments, although Pat so far had been unable to come up with a man that interested her friend more than a fleeting few minutes.

Lately, Katie had been toying with the idea of expanding the shop—throwing open all the rooms, or most of them, and taking an apartment next door. It was a big move, and would require a mortgage, taking on extra help, perhaps even a partner. The trade was there, but the idea scared her to death. Right now she made enough to get by, but if she was ever to have a comfortable margin, extras, time off for an occasional vacation, she was going to have to expand. She was considering asking Pat if she would like to buy into the shop.

'Hi!'

Pat, with Trisha trailing her, looked brisk and cheery. Mother and daughter were much alike—full of self-confidence and drive. Trisha had the advantage of more than just a year's seniority over Kim. She was smarter, quicker, taller, although of course that picture would change as they grew older.

Katie, emerging from the back with Kim, saw that Pat was dressed for work, in the long, colourful muu-muu they both wore in the store.

'I may as well warn you that Trisha is counting on a picnic. I hope you had it in your plans.' Pat surveyed Katie, who was wearing a skirt of faded denim and a red shirt instead of her usual shorts and jeans when she had the afternoon off. 'Oh, no,' she said doubtfully, 'I can see you aren't.'

'But I am,' Katie broke in hastily at the look on Trisha's face. 'I have one little errand to do first, honey, then we'll go to the beach.'

Trisha, who was wearing shorts and carrying her pail and shovel, grinned with relief.

'Errand? Shopping?'

Since there was no reason to make a mystery of it, Katie said briefly, 'No. I want to see a showing at Fine Galleries of a—collection of paintings. By Sacha Kimberly.' It was the first time she had said the name aloud since Aunt Anna's death, and it felt strange on her lips.

Pat's reaction was uninterest. 'Sorry. I'm a peasant myself. I don't know the slightest thing about art. But it's your thing, isn't it, Katie? Why not leave the kids here with me until you're through, so you can see it in peace?'

Katie struggled briefly with the temptation, then reluctantly withstood it. Later she was to wonder bitterly what would have been the outcome if she had followed Pat's suggestion. 'You might get busy and they'd be in the way. No, I'll take them and leave them in the car outside the Galleries. I won't be in there long.'

On the way out Katie gave the little shop a last final look as she always did before leaving it. It was a pleasure to know that everything she saw was her own, and had been got through her own efforts and hard work. She was supplied by a small, reliable list of craftsmen to whom she paid good returns for good work. She was too far off the beaten track to appeal to the average tourist, so that meant she had to depend on returnees, or customers who were willing to pay for specialized articles that were handcrafted locally.

One room was devoted exclusively to children's things— exquisite little handmade bonnets with deep brims and enormous bouffant crowns, smocked baby dresses, delicately crocheted blankets, wooden toys. There were stuffed animals and rag dolls with painted faces and a profusion of baby pillows, each a confection of lace and ruffles, tossed with careless abandon into a Victorian baby stroller. The other room was filled with an assortment of items designed to appeal to adults with tastes for anything from rope hammocks, baskets, pottery and plants, woven and quilted items, wind chimes, jars of preserved ginger and pineapple, to a wide range of sketches and watercolours by local talent.

'Quit gloating over the merchandise and get out of here.'

Pat's voice was goodnatured behind her. 'Go on and enjoy yourself!'

The Julian Fine Galleries was on a broad, palm-lined street filled with exclusive shops selling expensive items. Katie was no stranger to it—in line with her work, she had met Julian casually several times, and knew him to be a pleasant man who was fanatically devoted to promoting talented artists.

She was fortunate to find a parking place directly in front of the building. Leaving the children in the car with Sammy on guard, she manoeuvred herself out of the cramped seat of the little Volkswagen. There was a drinks machine at the corner, and she brought them two cans of soda, then, with a final admonition, 'Don't talk to strangers,' she left them with a promise to hurry.

The smoothly modern front of the Galleries was in keeping with the decor of the street, with potted palms at the entrance to a tiny courtyard and a lacy ironwork balcony overhanging the double front doors. Inside, the interior was cool, dim and luxurious, with muted blues and greys predominating in the carpet and curtains. Already the gallery was comfortably filled, the discreet murmur of voices mingling with the piped-in music. The fashionable silver-haired woman manning the telephone desk at the entrance boredly waved Katie towards the Kimberly rooms upon her enquiry.

Katie was unprepared for her reaction when she saw the first painting, *Country Girl*—a windswept sky, a cabin and a long hill yellow with sunflowers. And a girl she knew to be herself. Leaning forward, she read the neatly printed card, 'Property of the artist'. She drew a shaky breath. He had not sold it. But if this was the way she was going to react, she had better not try to see the rest of the paintings. Cautiously she glanced around the gallery, but was reassured to see that nothing else seemed familiar to her.

Striving for composure, Katie moved on. There were about twenty paintings in all, covering the walls of three rooms. There were no prices, of course, for none of them were for sale, but she knew that each square of canvas and oil represented thousands of dollars. Not that Sacha needed the money. Her mouth twisted. As the heir to the Tillotson millions, he would never have to starve in a garret, or sell his paintings to pay the rent, as many of his fellow artists did. He had always been unduly sensitive to the fact that his circumstances were so different from theirs, so much so that very few of them had any idea of his background. She herself had been in the dark about Sacha when they were married. It had taken Irene West to enlighten her that she had married a rich man.

But no one could deny that he could paint. Money hadn't given him his talent, and he had earned every scrap of praise wrung from the hostile critics, reluctant to give him any credit. As Katie studied them, she saw a depth of richness and perception that grew with each canvas, and for the first time she began to appreciate the full scope of Sacha's genius.

In the last gallery, a group of people were viewing the highlight of the showing, the award-winning *Dreaming*. It was a portrait of a woman who sat dreamily combing her hair by the light from an open window. She was half naked, and the light shone on her raised arms and full breasts, outlining them with rich detail. The portrait had been pronounced erotic, not because of the subject matter, but the sensuality of the woman's expression. Her face literally glowed with sated passion.

'Dear God,' thought Katie frantically, 'is this how he saw me?'

She had never seen the finished portrait and she was in a panic lest she be recognised. She had read the controversy

at the time of the Award—Sacha had admitted that the
portrait was of his wife—but at the time, studying the
crude newspaper reprints, she did not think it resembled
her. Now, it seemed glaringly obvious. She looked at the
other people covertly. No one was noticing her, but instinctively her only thought was of flight.

She shied backwards, bumping into the opening door of
Julian Fine's office as she did so. A tall, dark-haired man
was emerging at the same time, saying over his shoulder,
'Until Monday, then, Julian.' He automatically reached
out to catch her as they collided and she looked directly
into dark, astonished eyes.

'Katie!'

Katie pivoted frantically, desperate to get away, and as
she turned, her temple struck a corner of the door—hard.
She crumpled, feeling the arms holding her tighten. When
she recovered consciousness she was lying on a couch in
Julian Fine's office. She recognised the furnishings, and
Julian's big, square desk opposite. And there was Julian
himself, perched upon the edge, his pleasant, homely face
wrinkled with anxiety. As soon as he saw her eyes open, he
asked solicitously, 'Are you all right, Mrs Lockwood? Do
you need a doctor?'

'I—I don't think so,' she said unsteadily. So far as she
could tell, they were alone. 'I think I'll be all right.'

She started to push herself upright on her elbows when a
brown hand and slim, tapering fingers appeared out of
nowhere and pushed her firmly back upon the sofa pillow.
Katie caught a glimpse of a gold watch band half hidden
by springing black hairs before the hand disappeared.

'Lie still!' Sacha said sternly. 'We don't know if you're
all right or not. We may have to call a doctor yet.'

Obediently Katie lay still, frozen with shock, her half-
open eyes watching as he placed a damp towel on her
forehead. As Sacha leaned forward she closed her eyes

abruptly, her nostrils assailed by a combination of remembered odours that meant Sacha—the spicy tang of his
shaving lotion and the subtle, yet familiar, scent of clean
male flesh.

Yet he had changed. For one thing, instead of his usual
paint-stained jeans, he was wearing a crisp grey business
suit that fitted his tall, supple frame like a glove, and she
had caught a glimpse of a dark red silk tie and pale blue
cuffs before she closed her eyes. His hair was shorter, too,
barely covering the top of his ears and clearing his collar
behind. Katie was amazed at how comprehensive her brief
look had been, but it was as though every nerve ending in
her body was registering impressions.

'Julian,' her heart quivered at the sound of the deep
tones, then steadied, 'would you be good enough to allow
me to talk privately to Katie for a minute?'

'Katie?'

'Yes. Mrs—Lockwood. We're old friends.'

'Of course.'

Even the sound of the closing door was reluctant. Julian
must be dying of curiosity, but he knew better than to
protest, thought Katie, just as she did. She knew Sacha too
well. If he intended to talk to her, then he would do it,
either here or elsewhere, so it had better be here. Closing
her eyes tightly, she reminded herself that she merely
had to remember not to fly into a panic and lose her
head.

'Sit up if you like.' Sacha sounded as though he did not
believe in her faintness. 'If your head spins, put it back,
but I think a little of Julian's good brandy will get the
colour back into your cheeks.'

Katie's hand stole to her cheeks, then she cautiously
raised her head and swung her feet on to the floor. She felt
weak but not dizzy. Sacha removed the towel from her
forehead, then handed her a tumbler half filled with a

golden liquid. Their fingers touched fleetingly and Katie flinched from the resultant electric shock as though she had been bitten.

As she sipped the brandy she studied him through her lashes. The change was more than merely a suit instead of his habitual blue jeans or a shorter haircut. New, deeper lines had been added to his face, and his mouth looked taut and bitter, as though he had often been unhappy. There was even a brush of grey at his temples. What had happened to make him look so hard? Had his affair with Irene turned out badly? Or was there now someone else? Divorce was so easy nowadays, as Katie had reason to know. Perhaps Sacha was even married now. There would be someone, she knew, for a man as handsome and virile as Sacha did not lack for feminine companionship, for a— sleeping partner. However, he did not like brief, one-night episodes; he had once told her that one of the best things about their marriage was waking up and finding her in bed beside him.

Deliberately, Katie slammed the door on her memories and looked up, suddenly aware that he was studying her just as intently as she was him.

'Well?' she asked defiantly. 'Have I changed?'

'Yes. Superficially, it's nothing more than that you're wearing your hair loose instead of braided as you used to do. And your—er—outline is rounder and more feminine.' His eyes narrowed speculatively. 'But there's more, too. You seem older and more mature.'

'Even I eventually grew up.' Her voice was brittle.

'What are you doing here?' he asked patiently, ignoring the little dig.

'Looking at your exhibit,' she said brightly. 'I read about it in the papers and I wanted to see it. Just curiosity, you understand,' she added airily, 'for old times' sake. The paper didn't mention that you would be here.'

'I didn't care to have it publicised,' he said briefly. 'I'm staying on a ranch on the island of Hawaii. But that isn't what I meant, and you know it,' he added harshly. 'I want to know what you're doing *here*, in Honolulu. I searched San Francisco and the entire state of California for you, but it never occurred to me you'd do such a harebrained thing as leave the mainland!'

Katie stared at him blankly. 'Searched? Why?'

'*Why?*' He sounded angry, almost violent. 'Surely you realise that I was concerned for you? You were my wife; you didn't draw any money from our account, and none of your friends had heard from you! In fact, you literally vanished off the face of the earth after you signed the papers in Martin's office! Naturally he expected you to return to the apartment, and *I* certainly did. I didn't try to get in touch with you at first, thinking I'd give you time—— Anyway, it was ten days before either of us realised that you were missing.'

'Oh.' Katie sipped the brandy and although it burned like fire going down, she was cold. This was worse, much worse than she had imagined it would ever be. 'I'm sorry you were inconvenienced,' she said carefully. 'I assumed that no one would care if I went away after I signed the divorce papers.'

'The hell you did!' Sacha said bitterly. 'You must have known damned well that I'd be concerned about you.'

'I l-left a note,' she faltered.

'And it told me exactly nothing! A few polite words writing me out of your life. But never mind that now. You're here, and I want to know why you came here, to Hawaii. You and your parents always lived near San Francisco.'

Katie was bewildered. He sounded almost accusing, as though he suspected her of some ulterior motive in coming to Hawaii. So far as the other was concerned—his assertion that he had been concerned about her—she was not surprised about that. Sacha's conscience might have troubled him after she left, although she would have thought he'd be too relieved to be rid of her so painlessly to worry overmuch about her. But he had always acted as though she was dimwitted, needing guidance. Even now—wings of panic beat in her throat at the thought of what he might discover if he persisted. She finished her brandy and put her glass down carefully, the action giving her a breathing space in which to think of what she must say.

'I've been here five years,' she said mildly, 'and doing very nicely, too, thank you. My only living relative, my mother's sister Anna, lived here, and when she learned of Dad's death, she wrote and asked me to come and live with her. The letter was a long time in reaching me, for the only address she had was the one we had when Mother was alive, and finally it was forwarded to the Institute and then on to me. As a matter of fact, I—I—got the letter the day that I—you—we split up. That's why I didn't mention it to you.' As I was in the habit of doing, babbling every single thing, every secret, every thought I ever had, thereby boring you to tears, no doubt. 'Afterwards,' Katie added, her throat so tight that she got out the words with difficulty, 'Hawaii seemed like a good place to go.'

He must know why. He must know that she couldn't have stayed on and watched him with Irene. He had been studying her closely as she stammered out her wretched little story, and now he asked abruptly, 'Julian said you were a widow. Is that true? If so, why are you calling yourself by your maiden name?'

Her mind frantically jiggled dates, years, before she reluctantly came to the conclusion that she had better stick to the truth, more or less. Sacha would be quick to spot any discrepancy if she tried to lie too elaborately.

'Aunt Anna preferred for her friends to think that I

was—a widow, rather than a divorcee. She was old-fashioned that way.'

He raised his eyebrows quizzically but did not press the point. 'Was?' he asked gently. 'She's dead, then?'

'Yes. I—we had a little shop, together. Since her death I run it alone.'

'So Julian said.' He had been leaning against the desk, and now he stood up abruptly. 'Well, if you're feeling better, let's go.'

'Go? Go where?' Katie asked blankly.

'To your place. A restaurant. Any place where we can talk,' he added impatiently.

'Talk? Why do we need to talk? I've told you everything about myself you need to know!' Her voice rose shrilly.

'Not everything,' Sacha said dryly. 'If you think I intend to let it go at this, you're mistaken, Katie. You've just had a bad experience and you shouldn't be allowed to drive—or walk—home alone. Do you have a car, by the way?' Her straw handbag had been lying on the desk, and he picked it up and casually thrust his hand in, as though he had a perfect right to explore its capacious interior. 'What the hell is this?' He dug up the wrapped package of peanut butter sanwiches. 'Is this your lunch? Were you planning to eat across the street in the park? Or—ah! Car keys!' They dangled from his fingers. 'I'll have Julian move your car to the parking lot behind this building. It's for the Galleries staff. We'll go in my car.'

Katie stood up abruptly and reached frantically for her keys. In the back of her mind danced a vision of two small children and a little dog patiently waiting outside in her car. She was appalled—and frightened—at the easy way Sacha had taken charge of her. 'Give them to me!' she cried. 'I'm not going anywhere with you! I—I'll meet you later if you insist, but for now——'

'What's the matter, Katie?' he taunted. 'Were you

meeting a man after lunch? Or was he sharing your sandwiches with you? I'm sorry, but he'll have to cool off his ardour under a cold shower until I deliver you to him.'

Katie was too panicky to resent the insinuation. 'There's no man! It's merely—that is, I have a shop to run and—and—I have to get back to it,' she protested. The thought of Sacha sticking determinedly to her side through some preverse desire to thwart a man he imagined she was meeting made her giddy with apprehension.

'Fine,' he said smoothly. 'I'd like to see your little place, Katie. On second thoughts, we'll take your car and I'll return here in a taxi to pick up mine.'

He seemed to sense her desire to get away, and Katie saw, with a sinking heart, that she had no hope of shaking him. He was already leading her inexorably towards the door, and she knew that once they walked out of the front door of the Galleries they would be hailed delightedly by the children. She had to delay and hope she could slip away while his attention was diverted.

What would have happened if she had been successful, she never knew, for they were interrupted by an agitated tapping at the door, and it was flung open by Julian's elegant receptionist, who was looking, at the moment, slightly flustered.

'Mrs Lockwood, there are two children and a dog out here looking for you,' she said fussily. 'I—that is, Mr Fine said to ask you if——' Before she could make it clear what Julian had said to ask, however, the very thing that Katie had been at such pains to prevent—the nightmare that she had been trying to avoid—happened.

Kim and Trisha, the little girl holding a struggling Sammy in her arms, erupted into the room, almost under the skirts of the indignant receptionist. Kim darted forward to hug his mother's knees just as Trisha dropped Sammy who promptly gave a flying leap into Katie's arms, that automatically opened to receive him.

'We waited and waited, Aunt Katie, but she wouldn't let us come in!' She glared at the receptionist who sniffed audibly as she slammed the door behind them. 'And then Kim 'sisted he was sick!'

The little boy raised an eager face and beamed at her. 'I *was*, Mommy!' he said with devastating clarity. 'I was sick! An' I wanted to see the pictures, too. You don't mind, do you, Mommy?' he added coaxingly.

'Mommy? Katie, who—who is this?' Sacha's voice was hoarse and ragged as his disbelieving eyes met hers.

Katie swallowed convulsively. She had always known that this moment would come some day—it had been part of her worst nightmares. Now that it was here she was defenceless, helpless to stem the tide of rushing events. She squared her shoulders bravely and managed to speak through trembling lips. 'Kim's—my son.'

She was not unprepared for the awful blaze of anger that lit his eyes, but nevertheless, his words shocked her by their savagery.

'And mine! You bitch!' he ground out between clenched teeth. 'I could kill you for this!'

CHAPTER TWO

KATIE's first thought was to get the children out of the way before Sacha said anything more. She called them to the outer door, all the while trying desperately to keep the strain out of her voice.

'Children, come here! There's a garden out there with a fountain in the centre—see? And a big fish, a dolphin, with a boy riding on its back. W-will you play in the garden with—with Sammy while I talk to the man?' she chattered glibly. Sacha loomed up menacingly behind her and she froze. Kim had not noticed the odd tone of her voice, but she saw Trisha watching her curiously.

Katie knew about the garden. It was very private, and enclosed by a brick wall, and could be reached only through the Galleries. Julian often used it as a background for the elegant little wine and cheese parties he gave for visiting celebrities. Katie had attended such a party once herself. She was fumbling nervously with the door catch when Sacha's hand stopped her.

'I'll take the children out,' he said harshly. 'I want to speak to my—Kim—if you please.'

After that Katie had no choice but to remain inside, watching painfully as the man led the children towards the fountain. She had always known that Sacha would know Kim was his once he saw the boy. His artist's eye would see the bone structure, the eyes, the shape of the head—oh, there were a thousand and one clues! And he was calling the tune now, and he was angry. She quivered at the thought of an angry, resentful Sacha. From the window she saw him drop to his haunches before Kim and speak. Kim replied, waving his arms, his little face gleaming with curiosity, but Sacha's answer, when it came, apparently shook him, for Katie saw the little thumb creep slowly to his mouth. She almost broke down then. Hot tears filled her eyes and spilled over, scalding her cheeks. She fumbled for a tissue and wiping her eyes when Sacha returned.

'Damn you, Katie, he's mine, isn't he?' he flung at her in a low, savage voice.

'Sacha, I—I——' She stopped, unable to go on.

'I asked his name—my own son! I had to ask his name! You even had the umitigated gall to name him for me, didn't you? Yet you stopped short of letting me know you were pregnant. What did you do—label him a bastard?'

She shuddered, her shoulders hunched defensively under the hail of angry words. 'No. He—he's—you're down on the birth certificate as his father. His name is Sacha Kimberly.'

'Well, that makes things easier,' he grated, 'but it comes a long way from making up to me for the four lost years of my son's life! Why didn't you tell me you were having my baby?'

Katie dropped her head, then crossed her arms helplessly over her chest. Standing before him this way, she felt like a prisoner before the bar. With an exasperated exclamation Sacha gripped her shoulders and gave her a shake that brought her head bobbing up to meet his.

'I asked you a question, damn you!' His eyes were black pools of anger. 'Didn't I have a right to know you were carrying my child?'

A long shudder rippled through Katie's body and he tightened his grip, as though he felt her desperate urge to get away. 'Did you know before you left San Francisco that you were pregnant?'

Briefly, Katie considered the possibility of lying to him,

but discarded it for the truth. 'Yes,' she said baldly.

His mouth tautened to a harsh gash and he almost threw her away from him. 'Yet you left anyway, you little bitch, and put me through hell looking for you, wondering if you were alive or dead! Why?' He almost spat the words at her.

Katie's voice trembled. 'I was going to tell you th-that night when you returned from New York. Y-you remember, you called me from Kennedy, so I w-went out, bought wine and candles for a celebration dinner—but when you got in you asked me at once for a divorce.' She glanced away, her face hardened by the remembered pain. 'I—didn't think about the baby at first, but when I did I knew I must have someone of my own. And I didn't think you would care,' she added desolately.

Sacha's face was inscrutable as he listened. 'Didn't it occur to you that I wouldn't have wanted a divorce if I'd know about the baby?'

'No.'

'Most women would have thought of that at once.'

Katie could have told him she was not like most women. She had never been clever about men and hadn't the slightest idea how to keep one who was growing tired of her. She had been too open about her feelings and when she was hurt, which was often, she struck out with wild accusations of unfaithfulness, threw scenes and tantrums and cried. In other words, she did all the wrong things. She had made such a scene before the New York trip, but then, after she learned about the baby, it seemed as though everything was going to be all right. Until Sacha returned, requesting a divorce. It had shocked and frightened Katie into begging for another chance. Even now, the memory of her abject pleading seared her with humiliation. His refusal had been curt, abrupt, even harsh, but he must indeed wonder why she hadn't used her pregnancy to bludgeon him into staying, not knowing it had been that final weary, bored utterance, 'Please, for God's sake don't let me have to listen to you beg. I'd like to remember you as having a little dignity,' that had stopped cold every wild promise trembling on her lips.

She had let him go without another word, watching silently as he packed the rest of his things. Then, not looking at her, he told her that she should see his lawyer the next day, and if she wanted anything at all she was to ask Martin for it. She could almost hear his unspoken words, 'And don't bother me!' She had thought of the baby then, but by that time he was gone, and after a sleepless night she had remembered Aunt Anna's letter.

Shrugging slightly, as though touched by the memory of the brutal way he had dismissed her, Sacha said, 'Very well, Katie, let's forget it. I'm as much to blame as you. Anyway, we have the future to think of now, and the son we've made between us. We have to talk, come to some understanding. I intend to have a share in my son's life, and for a start, I want him told *right now* that I'm his father. He asked my name and when I told him it was the same as his, he was confused.' Katie remembered the small, bewildered thumb. 'Will you tell him or shall I?'

'You—do it. I don't think I can,' she said tightly.

'Very well. Where were you gong from here?'

'To the beach. The shop—Trisha's mother works for me at the shop on Wednesdays.' She swallowed nervously.

'Then we won't disappoint them. We'll go to the beach.' His eyes rested thoughtfully on her drooping figure. 'Is that why you had the food with you? It was to be a picnic?'

'Yes.'

He raked impatient fingers through his hair. 'Then I'd better arrange something if I'm to get some lunch,' he said ruefully. 'I'll call the children in now.'

Kim's reaction to the news that Sacha was his father was enthusiastic. 'You mean my very own daddy?' he asked, round-eyed.

Sacha was kneeling beside him. 'Your very own daddy,' he assured him solemnly. 'You may call me Daddy if you like.'

Kim looked blissfully at Trisha. 'Will you come to see me on Sundays like Trisha's daddy does?'

'I'll see you a lot more than just Sundays. In fact, from now on, I intend to see you all the time,' Sacha added deliberately, glancing at Katie coolly.

Kim threw his arms around his father's neck and Katie caught her breath on a sharply drawn gasp. She knew a sudden piercing pang of jealousy as sharp as a knife-thrust to the stomach, and knew from the cold mockery in Sacha's eyes that he was perfectly aware of what she was feeling. But why not? she thought resentfully, even as she flushed with shame. Jealousy might be a demeaning emotion, but it was certainly a natural one. Hadn't she been Kim's rock and anchor since he was born? She had been mother, father and family to him. Now, suddenly, another person had appeared, filling his horizon temporarily—another parent—and it hurt a little to watch how quickly Kim accepted the change.

'A daddy! A daddy!' he chanted almost to himself. 'I've been wanting a daddy so-o-o long!' He gave a sigh of deep satisfaction.

Sacha stood up, Kim still clinging to his neck. 'Did you know he felt like this?' he demanded accusingly.

Katie swallowed nervously but said nothing.

Sacha's faced darkened. 'That means you did! God, Katie, I could——!' He stopped abruptly, suddenly conscious of the child he was holding. His mouth tightened. 'Are you ready to go?'

'Yes.'

Trisha's little hand slid forlornly into hers, a very subdued little Trisha, who until now had had one vast advantage over Kim. Now she was feeling rather lost and left out, and Katie knew exactly what her emotions were at the moment. She gave her hand a sympathetic squeeze, then, calling to Sammy, she picked up the little dog and with Trisha, followed Sacha out. Fortunately, the gallery was empty except for Julian, who stood murmuring to his receptionist. From the sidelong glance he directed at her, Katie knew he had already recognised her as the model for *Dreaming*.

Sacha handed him her car keys. 'Julian, would you be so good as to have my wife's car parked until I can have it picked up?'

Katie was taken aback, too surprised for a minute at his choice of words to appreciate Julian's quandary. Julian had wondered about her exact status, for of course, being no fool, he remembered the controversy at the time of the Award. There had been a lot of discussion about the artist's estranged wife and more than one reporter had wondered openly about her disappearance. Sacha had refused to comment, so the press had been forced to draw its own conclusions. There had been some speculation that she might be dead. And Julian, being from the art world, would remember all that as well as the fact that Katie Lockwood had been calling herself a widow all these years and had a child. That it was Kimberly's child was beyond dispute. But why had the famous artist said that she was his wife, instead of his ex-wife? Presumably because she *was* his wife, and in the conversation that had just been conducted behind the closed doors of his office, they had come to terms. He had made his peace with his estranged wife. Julian would have given his soul to know what went on during that reconciliation—he could have sold the story ten times over to the gossip columns—but as it was, he had the scoop of the year so far as the art world and Honolulu was concerned, and it was going to do his Galleries no harm either.

So he came forward with a wide, beaming smile and said easily, 'Nonsense, Sacha, I'll see to it that the car is returned to Mrs Kimberly's shop at once.'

Outside, Sacha settled the children and Sammy in the back seat of a silver-grey Mercedes, then held the front door open for Katie. Previously he had owned a low-slung Lamborghini, but this discreetly luxurious car seemed to fit his new image.

They made one stop, at Carlo's, a famous restaurant that Katie knew of by reputation but had never been inside. The parking lot was filled, but Sacha waved away the attendant and pulled into an empty slot.

'I won't be long,' he promised as he unbuckled his seat belt.

He wasn't, for within a few minutes he was back, carrying a picnic basket, and followed by a waiter with a table-cloth draped over one arm and a cooler under the other.

'What's this?' asked Katie.

'A picnic,' he explained briefly. With the waiter's help, he saw to the storage of the basket and cooler, then handed the man a note that had him still smiling and bowing as they drove away.

He seemed to know just where he wanted to go. Passing Waikiki, he headed for a deserted stretch of white sand that was sheltered from the wind by a line of palm trees. It was such a beautiful place that in spite of herself, Katie felt herself relaxing, responding to its soothing restfulness.

The only jarring note was Sacha. She felt herself tightening with nerves every time he came near, or even spoke, and she was as aware of him as she had been in the days of their marriage, except that this time her feelings were mixed with dread and apprehension. He seemed unconscious of her fear-filled eyes as he dumped their gear, then called the children to him and added coolly, 'I'm taking them along the beach to hunt for shells. Why don't you spread out the lunch while we're gone?'

She watched them go uneasily, watched Kim slip a confiding hand into his father's. What was Sacha asking him, asking them both, for Trisha was doing her share of the talking? Of course, there was a battle building up, and Katie knew that Sacha was no longer going to allow her full custody of his son. Apparently he was not married, at least at the present time; hence his casual reference to her as 'his wife' to Julian. And she felt sure that Sacha was not going to allow Kim to remain in Hawaii while he lived on the mainland—which meant that her little shop, her independent life, was gone, for of course, wherever Kim went she would have to go, too. Desperately she considered the alternatives. She would just have to wait and see.

She turned to the picnic basket. Everything that could possibly be wanted on a picnic was there. Sandwiches, crusty fried chicken, a foil-lined box of potato salad, another of fruit salad, raw vegetable snacks, caviar—an item that raised her eyebrows slightly—strawberries, peaches, and ice cream cups packed away in ice. And in the cooler was lemonade and beer. And neatly folded in the snowy white tablecloth were napkins and a package of wet wipes. Nothing could have been a greater contrast to her own picnic plans of soggy sandwiches and cans of soda on a crowded beach.

The children fell upon the food with whoops of pleasure, when they returned, while Katie continued her musings. Sacha wanted Kim. Moreover, Kim had needs that Sacha was more than willing to supply, and Sacha had money and could afford a longdrawn-out custody case. Kate couldn't. It was as simple as that.

Just knowing that she was going to have to negotiate for

the most important thing in her life had brought on a headache that had Katie's temples pounding with a near-agonising pain. She made a small, betraying movement and he looked up. His eyes narrowed slightly on her pale face and he asked, 'What's the matter? Why aren't you eating your lunch?'

'I don't have your appetite,' she snapped nastily.

'Too bad,' he drawled blandly. 'Perhaps you don't have my clear conscience.'

He was laughing at her! Katie trembled with fury. 'Sacha, I've got to talk to you. This can't go on. We've got to discuss what we're going to do. I—I realise you have rights——'

'Kind of you,' he murmured sarcastically.

'But I'm Kim's mother,' she added awkwardly. 'My—my rights come before yours——'

He flicked a warning glance at her, but fortunately, just then, Sammy provided a diversion by snatching a drumstick from under Trisha's nose and scampering off down the beach with it, his two white ears flying like two little flags behind him. The children jumped up and pursued him, shrieking. Sacha turned to her quickly.

'Yes, I agree. We are going to have to talk, but not before the children. I don't want Kim disturbed until we come to terms, and Trisha seems to me like a young lady who would easily pick up a lot of loose information and repeat it. So we'll discuss it later, although I may as well tell you now, Katie, that I don't intend for my son to grow up as I did, with his time divided between two warring parents.'

'I gathered—from what you said to Julian—that you haven't remarried?' she murmured diffidently.

He did not reply for a long moment. 'No, I haven't,' he agreed cynically. 'Does that relieve your mind?'

She flushed. 'It—makes things easier. For the custody

thing, I mean. If there aren't any steparents. An—another wife would—might—resent Kim.'

'You're quite right,' he agreed smoothly. 'It *does* make things easier. I remember an occasional husband of my mother's getting into the battles between her and my father. She had six, you know—husbands. And my time spent with her was usually a battle with one of them for her attention. I don't intend to have that sort of thing for my son.'

'I have no plans to remarry,' Katie said stiffly, in case he was labouring under some sort of misconception. 'I—don't have the money to fight you in court, Sacha,' she added desperately, 'but I won't give him up.'

'I have a good idea of your financial situation, and the necessity to agree to my terms,' he drawled callously. 'You may not like them—in fact, you might as well prepare yourself to make sacrifices. If you want to discuss this now, I can send the kids down the beach and we can talk.'

'No!' Now that she was faced with it, Katie sought desperately to prolong their decision-making talk. 'I—I have an awful headache. C-can't we go home?'

Sacha glanced at her quickly and noticed her eyes were cloudy with pain. 'Why the hell didn't you say so earlier?' he asked roughly. 'I'm not a monster! I don't enjoy putting you through pain!'

He packed away their supplies efficiently, then whistled to the children and the dog. Unlike their usual ploy with Katie, they didn't argue when he told them crisply that they were returning home. Katie climbed limply into the front seat, and Sacha saw to fastening her seat belt before he closed the door on her, then strode around to the driver's side Before driving off, he turned partially in the seat and looked directly at her.

'You're worrying yourself sick, aren't you?' he asked. His voice was a blend of concern and exasperation.

Katie bit her lip. Tears rose to the surface and she blinked fiercely to hold them back. She couldn't speak at first, then, 'Shouldn't I be?'

'You were always a little noodle,' he said ruefully. 'You leap to conclusions and then you jump—straight into the frying pan! And then wonder why you're burned!'

'You're mixing your metaphors.' Her voice held a ghost of laughter.

He grinned. 'So I am. But before you start worrying yourself into a state of nervous collapse, suppose you wait until you hear what I have to say. It might be the solution to all our problems.'

Sacha's words had given Katie a slight glimmer of hope—not much, to be sure, but some. By the time they arrived home and Trisha had been packed off back to her mother, her headache was gone, eased by the wind in her face and the security of knowing that the children had obeyed without murmuring Sacha's order to be quiet. She had had to do no more than give her address, and Sacha had found his directions effortlessly—another indication that he knew more about Hawaii and Honolulu than she had first suspected.

Back home, the grey Mercedes looked out of place parked in the narrow driveway behind her shabby little Volkswagen. Sacha got out first, flexing his muscles tiredly and massaging his neck as though he, too, felt a need to release his tension. Katie watched him covertly, trying to guess his reaction to her little shop. A great deal would depend upon whether he thought it was a proper place to bring up a child, and he was looking at it inscrutably, a look that immediately put her on the defensive.

Katie was thankful that the interior of her shop needed no apology. With the lights on the glass shelves sparkling clean, it looked fresh and modern. Sacha glanced around appreciatively.

'Nice,' he commented lazily. 'Shall I carry him to bed for you?' he added, picking up Kim. The little boy had been rubbing his eyes, but at Sacha's words he stiffened and protested that he wasn't sleepy. However, his father dealt with that minor little rebellion with a single crisp command and followed Katie down the dingy back hallway.

Kim's bedroom was hot, small and cluttered with his toys. As Katie snapped on the small revolving fan, she wished despairingly that the air-conditioning that cooled the shop had been extended to the rest of the house. She sighed. As always, it had been a matter of money, but when Kim woke up, drenched with perspiration as he usually did, she had no doubt that Sacha would see it as another indication that she couldn't care for him properly. While she went through the preliminaries of getting him down for a delayed nap, Sacha stood at the window and looked out on the play yard in the back. Katie had made a valiant effort to keep the grass growing, but was only partially successful. There were a couple of stunted trees, a swing and a sandbox, but the whole was shadowed by the towering buildings on either side. She watched his mouth tighten ominously, but he said nothing, either about that or the airlessness of the bedroom.

Finally, after the ritual of the stuffed duck and the teddy bear had been observed, and Sammy, who had been waiting patiently beside the bed, had been settled at Kim's feet, Katie turned away to lead Sacha from the room.

'We can talk now, if you like,' she said uneasily.

'Talk?' Sacha sounded absolutely astonished. 'I can't talk on an empty stomach. I'd like something to eat first, if you don't mind.'

'Something to *eat*?' Katie asked blankly. 'You mean—again?'

'Well, you made me leave before I finished my lunch,'

he explained plaintively. 'Surely you want me in a good humour before we have that talk, don't you?'

Katie pinched her lips together. 'This way,' she snapped.

She led the way to the kitchen, small and crowded by the addition of a rolltop desk and a table that she used as a cutting table. Motioning Sacha irritably towards a chair, she opened the refrigerator door and peered inside. 'Would you like to have what I was planning for dinner tonight?' she asked sarcastically.

'That sounds fine,' he said easily.

Katie did not quite snort with indignation, but her back was rigid with it as she put eggs into a saucepan to boil before preparing a salad.

As she worked, she was aware that Sacha was watching her closely, and she was uneasily aware of the male magnetism he exerted by his mere presence. He had not changed; he still had sex appeal and charm going to waste, she thought dourly, and without the slightest scruples about using it whenever necessary. She looked up once and saw his dark eyes intent on her as she peeled eggs and sliced tomatoes. Good grief, she wondered in amazement, is he really hungry? Or is he curious to see if I've learned how to cook?

Finally it was ready. Sacha took a cautious mouthful, then smiled slightly.

'Congratulations,' he said dryly. 'You used to be a lousy cook.'

'Is that why you wanted lunch?' she asked suspiciously. 'To see if I could cook?'

He shrugged dismissively. 'Aren't you having anything?'

'I'm not hungry.'

His face darkened. 'What are you trying to do—starve yourself? You didn't eat a bite at the beach!'

To silence him, she put a small portion of the salad on her plate, then proceeded to push it aimlessly from one side to the other to disguise the fact that she wasn't eating. Sacha's mouth tightened, but he said nothing more, and as soon as he had finished, Katie rose quickly.

'I'm too nervous to eat. Let's get this settled.' She added reluctantly, 'I suppose we'd better talk in the living room.'

Viewing the small living room through Sacha's eyes, it looked dingy and depressing. A small black and white television set mingled with a coffee table, a sagging couch and a couple of over-stuffed chairs to provide the maximum amount of furniture, the room would hold. Limp curtains hung at the windows. The room had started life as a bed-room and it still looked out of kilter and overcrowded.

Katie dropped tiredly on to the couch and Sacha seated himself at the other end, his trousers tautening along the line of his muscular thighs as he casually crossed one leg over a knee and laid his hand on his ankle. Desperately anxious to appear equally at ease, Katie picked up a packet of cigarettes she kept on the table and lit one jerkily.

'You never used to smoke.' His narrowed eyes met hers through the defiant puff of smoke she exhaled.

'So what? I do now!' she replied sharply, then immediately took a firm hold on herself. This was absurd. She was taking everything he said as criticism. As for smoking, she almost never did unless she was nervous, so why try to pretend that she was a three-packet-a-day smoker? But why, she added defensively, did he have to be relaxed, when *she* was on pins and needles?

She stubbed out her cigarette angrily. 'Sacha! About this talk—what are we going to do?'

'I think we'd better clear up all extraneous material first,' he began easily.

'Extraneous material?' she asked blankly.

'Yes. Your marital status, for instance. Obviously you've

not remarried, but is there someone—some man—who's playing stepfather to my son?'

Katie gasped as the meaning of his words penetrated. 'How dare you?' Her face flamed. 'And if there is, what of it? You have Irene, haven't you?'

'Irene?' he asked, and she could have sworn he was astonished. 'You mean—Irene West? That poisonous girl friend of yours?'

'Certainly! Wasn't she the reason you wanted a divorce? Or have you forgotten that I found you in her apartment the next morning after having plainly slept there all night?'

'Yes, I had forgotten that,' he drawled. 'So that's how you figured it out? Poor Katie! No, I asked you for a divorce because I got tired of that tendency of yours to magnify every trifle into a sure thing and make scenes over nothing. I went over to Irene's that night to try to make some sense out of some of your accusations, and in the process, I learned something about that woman's influence over you. She kept you tied in knots with her hints and innuendoes, didn't she? We sat up half the night talking and she made a bed for me on the sofa. I spent the rest of the night fending off her advances. When you rang the doorbell, I was about to leave.'

'I thought—I thought——' she mumbled.

'You thought—as you always did—that she was my mistress,' he said dryly. 'No, Katie. But your best friend was about as faithful as a rattlesnake.'

'I know that—now,' Katie said dully.

'There may, then, be hope for you yet,' he said sardonically. 'However, none of this has anything to do with our present problem. I asked you once—do you have a lover?'

'And I refuse to answer that!' Katie flared. 'Just because we were once married, you have no right to pry into my business! I don't have to answer any of your questions.'

'Careful, Katie,' he warned softly. 'You're treading on dangerous ground. You either answer me here and now, or you'll find yourself answering a lawyer's questions in court.'

She stared at the grim lines of his face. 'Oh, all right!' she said sullenly. 'There's no one. I don't have a—a—lover. I haven't had anyone since I—left you. I've been too busy trying to earn a living for myself and my child,' she added defensively. 'There, does that answer your questions?'

'One of them,' Sacha replied with a slight smile. He had relaxed at her answer, and now he rubbed the back of his neck as though releasing tired muscles from their tightness. 'See how painless it was?' he added dryly. 'Things might have been complicated if you'd picked up a husband or even a lover in the past four years, but as it is, there are no impediments to our living together again. And think how much simpler it will be for Kim,' he added, ignoring her shocked gasp. A lazy forefinger trailed a tingling path across her cheek to the edge of her mouth where it delicately outlined the shape of her lips. 'Poor Katie,' he murmured provocatively. 'No man, eh? How you must have missed me. You can't have enjoyed living alone. Not you. You were always an accomplished little sensualist.'

Katie jerked away indignantly. 'How dare you suggest that I'm ready to fall into your arms like ripe fruit. You're a conceited egotist, Sacha Kimberly! I've learned to live alone and like it, and I've learned to take care of myself, too. I'm not some silly little girl who's falling all over you to take her to bed. I don't need you! I'm my own person, and if you think I intend to remarry you merely because it suits your plans, you're wrong!' she added furiously. 'We'll come to some other arrangement about Kim. I've learned that the only good marriage is an equal marriage, and by that token, ours was lousy.'

'Bravo,' he said ironically. 'You *have* grown up. There've been times today when I've thought you were still the old Katie, who was often a whining bore. I infinitely prefer your new independence. But make no mistake, Katie,' a steely note crept into his voice, 'I do not intend to put up with outright defiance.'

'You won't have to put up with anything!' she snapped angrily, 'I tell you, I will not remarry you!'

'My dear girl,' he said dryly, 'who said anything about remarriage?'

'You mean——?' She stopped, spluttering, then started again, on a rising note of outrage. 'You mean—if you *think* I'll enter into some kind of irregular arrangement with you—some kind of bohemian set up——' She stopped again, disconcerted by his laughter.

'Are you visualising our living in sin, Katie, with our son everyday witness to it?' he chuckled, his dark eyes alight with amusement. 'Haven't you listened to a word I've said today? Don't you understand what I want—what I intend to have—for my son?' He reached for her and jerked her around to face him. 'Let me tell you again, and this time, you listen!' he said sternly. 'I don't intend to be a casual, part-time father. We're going to be his parents, you and I, which means that we eat together, we sleep together, we have other babies. And in case your busy little mind is at work on how to get out of it—don't! We're still legally married.'

'Legally married?' Her face whitened. 'B-b-but I signed papers—the next morning——'

'And I had Martin drop the divorce eight days later,' he said impatiently. 'You would have learned it, if you'd stayed around long enough or left a forwarding address. No, we're very much married, Katie. Which means that Kim was born legitimately and I have every legal right to him. More so than most fathers, for you deserted me and kept his existence a secret from me for four years. I think a judge would hand him over to me if I cared to follow it up, so make no mistake, either you play ball with me or you lose your son. It's as simple as that. I want him, Katie. He's mine, and I'll fight for him if I have to,' he added deliberately.

Katie's throat grew dry with horror as she listened to the biting terms of his proposal and the alternative he threatened. 'No, you wouldn't!' she gasped. 'Surely you wouldn't do that to me?'

'Try me,' he replied calmly. 'Just try me and see. I'll do anything to get my own way. Haven't you told me so often enough?'

'But you—wouldn't take him away—from me?' she faltered. 'I—it would kill him to be parted from me.'

'No,' he corrected her coolly, 'it would kill you, Katie. He would adapt, particularly as I'd be giving him a father to take your place. I've been showing you all day how quickly he's taken to me and it's just about killed you, hasn't it? You've made him your life, haven't you?'

'Of course I have!' she cried distractedly. 'How can you sit there and talk about taking him away from me as though it was nothing? He's been mine since the day he was born. I—I can't give him up!'

'I've given you an alternative,' Sacha reminded her cruelly.

'What sort of alternative is that?' she demanded. 'I'm to submit to your terms——'

'Precisely. You're to submit—to become my wife in every sense of the word. It shouldn't be too hard,' he added sardonically. 'As I remember, we've always been able to communicate in the bedroom.'

Katie flushed. His words brought back memories that she would have preferred to forget, especially just now when she needed every ounce of self-control to keep Sacha from guessing how shaken she was. In spite of herself, however, her eyes brightened, and she could not prevent herself from saying, half provocatively, half sarcastically, 'Does that mean if I please you, I'll get time off for good behaviour?'

She should have known it would be a mistake to challenge Sacha. His eyes narrowed slightly on her curling lips. 'Are you trying to tell me that you'll find it a hardship to be married to me?' he asked smoothly.

With a gesture that was insultingly effortless, he reached out lazily and pulled her off balance. One lean, strong hand lightly clasped her wrists, rendering her hands ineffective, and the other held her immovable across his chest. After the first shock, Katie struggled wildly in an attempt to free herself, but soon gave up and lay helpless, panting, her face upturned to his. Beneath her cheek she could feel the rock-hard muscles of his chest, cushioned slightly by a thick growth of hair. 'You've admitted that you've had no one since you left me.' His eyes glinted slightly as he took in her flushed, startled face. 'That means you've gone hungry, and if I know my Katie, you're very hungry indeed. You were my wife too long for me to not remember just what turns you on, Katie. No matter how hard we fought. I could usually bring you around when we shut the bedroom door, couldn't I? Our sex life never gave us any trouble. I think we'll find a common meeting ground to patch up our differences.' His taunting words had their effect, and Katie began to struggle again, angrily impotent against his superior strength. She pulled desperately at his hand, seeking to free her wrists, but the loose grip tightened like a vice. He watched with a sort of cool curiosity the straining pressure of her upthrust breasts against the thin, red-checked cloth of her shirt, then, idly, he put out a tentative forefinger and brushed one of the taut points.

Katie reacted like a scalded cat. Her imprisoned wrists jerked spasmodically, and she shrank back against his chest.

'Let me go, Sacha!' she cried hoarsely.

'Oh, no.' He smiled slightly, but only with his lips. The dark eyes remained watchful. 'That's just what I won't do until I show you something about your own needs.' He gripped her hair roughly, dislodging most of her carefully placed pins and bringing a golden-brown cloud tumbling down about her shoulders. His strong, cruel fingers forced her to remain absolutely still as he studied her face thoroughly, his eyes roaming from the wide, frightened eyes to the tremulous mouth, before finally pausing to study a frantic pulse that was beating wildly at the base of her throat.

'Oh, God, please, Sacha——' she moaned desperately.

'You used to beg for my kisses like that,' he mocked, then his mouth covered hers with a suddenness that took her by surprise. She struggled briefly before she admitted herself the vanquished in the uneven battle. Helplessly, she could not stem the tide of passion that rose to meet his as he soon had her lips gentled beneath his own, stripping her inhibitions as skilfully as his hand explored the intimate contours of her body. A warm tongue, trailing a burning path from the corner of her mouth, paused at the delicate lobe of her ear while his plundering hand teased her breasts. Automatically, her body responded to his expertise and Katie could do nothing to stop it. She was drowning in a soft warm cocoon of darkness. Unable to stop herself, she lifted an arm and brought his face closer to hers.

Then, abruptly, Sacha withdrew his mouth and set her upright with jarring suddenness.

'Snap out of it, sweetheart! Our son is calling you.'

Katie blinked dazedly. She felt bereft, as though heaven itself had slipped from her grasp. Then she heard it—

Kim's plaintive 'Mommy!' a cry that usually had the power to drag her from the very depths of sleep; yet, in Sacha's arms, she had heard nothing. How long had he been calling? A slow tide of crimson covered her neck and face as she realised that her blouse was open, her bra hung loose and her taut nipples gave lie, if nothing else, to any claims she might make to being indifferent to Sacha. Moreover, he was watching her amusedly, and she knew that he hadn't missed a thing.

With a stifled gasp she jumped to her feet and flew from the room, her cheeks burning with shame. *Snap out of it, sweetheart!* At that moment she hated him. He had accomplished what he had set out to do—which was to prove to her that he could still summon a response from her willing body, even after five years. She reminded herself fiercely that although she had loved him desperately when she left him five years ago, he had not loved her. And nothing had changed. Dear God, she was right back where she started. It suited Sacha to take her back as his wife—because of Kim. And she must never forget that that was his reason. She knew now that she still loved him, but she couldn't allow him to know it. To love without hope of return was to become a slave. If he had an inkling that what she felt for him was anything but the most basic physical need, he would use it ruthlessly to his advantage, no matter how much he bruised her heart in the process. No! If she was going to survive in this marriage, and she had to survive, or lose Kim, she was going to have to hide her love with every weapon at her disposal.

CHAPTER THREE

KIM was sitting up in bed, waiting for her, and his first words revealed his fast growing dependence upon his father.

'Where's Daddy?' he demanded, with an edge of fear and uncertainty in his voice that tore at her heart. 'He hasn't gone, has he, Mommy? Please, Mommy, Daddy's s-s-still here, isn't he?'

'Of course he is,' she reassured the little boy. 'He's in the living room——' But she wasn't able to complete the sentence, for Kim was already out of bed and racing down the hall towards the living room, Sammy yipping excitedly at his heels.

If she had wanted her answer, Katie thought tiredly, she had it now. She followed Kim slowly. Sacha had already gained a place as a person necessary to his son's happiness, and she couldn't take that away from Kim any more than she could deny him her own love. But she was necessary too; basically, the age-old law of nature still held true—a child needed the love of both parents.

'Are you going to stay here with us, Daddy?' Kim was on his father's lap, there was something convulsive about the grip around his neck. 'Say you're going to live with us, Daddy! You're not going to leave, are you? Please! Mommy wants you to stay, too, don't you, Mommy?'

Sacha's eyes glinted as they met Katie's. 'Well, Mommy? Would you like me to stay?'

'It looks like it's all settled,' she said expressionlessly.

'Then we'd better leave soon,' he said briskly, 'if we're to get home before dark.'

'Home?' Katie asked blankly.

'I should say, to my father's home,' he corrected himself. 'He lives on a ranch on the island of Hawaii. While you're getting a couple of bags packed, I'll make arrangements to have a helicopter standing by.'

'B-but—your father? Paul Kimberley? I—I didn't know he lived here in Hawaii.'

Sacha shrugged. 'I gathered you didn't, or that your aunt hadn't mentioned it.'

'My aunt? Would she have known him?'

'She might have.' He was noncommittal. 'You said she'd lived here a long time, and he's well known locally. However, my mother is the newsworthy one, because she's the heiress. Dad only wants to be left alone to attend to his business. On the whole, he shuns publicity.'

'Has he always lived here?' asked Katie.

'Of course. He's a *kamaaina*.'

'A—*kamaaina*? You mean someone who's born here?'

'Yes. His ancestors, too. My grandmother is a native Hawaiian. You'll meet her, too, because she lives with my father. My grandfather is dead. He was one of the early white settlers on the Island.' He grinned narrowly. Poor Katie! You fled me as though I was a devil, only to arrive at the homeland of my ancestors.'

She shrugged. 'How would I know?' she demanded bitterly. 'You never talked about yourself. Everything I know about you I learned from the newspapers or other people.'

'Are you rebuking me?' he asked wryly. 'I'm afraid I tried to avoid unpleasant subjects during the brief, halycon days of our marriage. The memories of the battles my parents fought over me were all too bitter for me to want to dwell on them. And I had other things to think about those days.'

'Yes. You reminded me that our conversation was mostly

confined to the bedroom,' she agreed tonelessly.

'Better that than the courtroom,' he reminded her dryly. 'From now on, I shall try to satisfy your curiosity, Katie. There'lbe no more secrets between us. You asked about my father — he's a rancher, with a cattle spread in Hawaii. He also raises pineapples, orchids and coffee, and prefers outdoor life to an office, but inevitably, has to involve himself in a certain amount of business. He didn't remarry after his divorce, and my grandmother, who's a very formidable old lady, oversees the running of his house.' He paused and looked at her speculatively, as though struck by a thought. 'Does that make a difference?'

'What?'

'That my grandmother is a Hawaiian.'

Katie stared at him uncomprehendingly, then suddenly understanding, flushed. 'I'm not a racist, Sacha.'

'I just wondered,' he said mildly.

'Have you been living here since—since I left?' The question had been nagging at her from the beginning.

He frowned. 'No. I've been back here often, and I spent a year on Kauai painting. I know Julian very well, Katie. How do you think he was able to prevail upon me to have the show here?'

'The paper said Mrs Wetherell persuaded you.'

He laughed shortly. 'No. The reporter got that little piece of misinformation from Claire, or perhaps Julian, who thought it made good publicity. Can you imagine the hell of knowing that my son has been on this island since his birth,' he added, with brutal abruptness, 'so close, yet I didn't know? God, I could kill you when I think of how I've missed the first four years of his life!'

'Mommy? Daddy?' Kim's anxious little face showed that he was aware of the deliberate note of cruelty in his father's voice.

Sacha hugged him and said lightly, 'How about it, Kim?

Shall we visit your grandfather's ranch? There's a swimming pool.'

'I can't swim,' Kim said doubtfully.

'Then you'll have to learn,' his father said briskly. 'You
can't be a *kamaaina* without knowing how to swim.'

'Then you plan to remain in Hawaii?' Katie asked carefully.

Sacha did not answer directly. 'Even if I didn't, Kim
would still be a *kamaaina*, because he was born here, just as
his father was,' he said evasively. 'Incidentally, I would
prefer you not to get into a discussion on this subject with
my grandmother. She's old and opinionated, and she wants
me to live at home—with her—on Hawaii.'

'B-but how can I keep my shop if you live on Hawaii?'
Katie faltered, dismayed.

'You can't. I suggest that while we're at my father's
house you see about having it put on the market. My
father employs a good firm of lawyers who can handle the
details for you, if you'd like.'

'Put my shop on the market? I won't! I've worked too
hard building it up just to—to abandon it like that!' she
sputtered.

'My dear Katie, what else do you expect to do?' he
asked patiently. 'No matter where you live, you're going
to be too busy to run a shop. Even if you found someone to
do it for you, I have no intention of allowing you to supervise it. Far better to put it on the market now before it
starts to go downhill and sell it while it's a going concern.
But of course, you may do just as you like. It's your shop,
after all, and if you want to walk off and leave it, it's your
business.'

Which meant, of course, that the shop would be worth-
less if she did. Sacha was right about that. And she had a
shrewd idea he would prefer her to do just that, for the few
thousands of dollars that this house and the contents of the

shop would bring meant nothing to him, but to her they represented a kind of independence.

'I'll sell it,' she muttered sullenly.

Once having the decision made for her to sell the shop, it was almost as though fate stepped in to take a hand, making it possible to sell Katie's Place overnight—to Pat Merritt. She came flying over as Katie was wandering helplessly around her bedroom, trying to put things together in a suitcase. Sacha had proven himself surprisingly competent by offering to bath Kim while she packed, and had then proceeded to push up his sleeves and with a minimum of splashing, get the little boy in and out of the bathtub in record time. Katie had left him to it, a little disturbed by the intimacy of Sacha in her bedroom and bathroom. She had lived alone too long; it was vaguely unsettling to have him bring a naked, wriggling little Kim into her bedroom and towel him dry.

Once Kim was powdered and pyjamaed, Sacha paused, his hands resting lightly on lean hips.

'Don't worry too much about packing,' he drawled. 'You can buy what you need on Hawaii. As for the rest of this stuff,' his eyes flicked the cheap bedroom furniture contemptously, 'I presume it will go with the shop?'

Katie looked up sharply, spoiling for a fight, stung by his offhand disimissal of what she had taken so long to build up. Her life's work. And this was her home, and whatever he might think of it, it had some value to her! But she stopped short, biting her lips, when she saw that he was waiting for the angry words that were trembling on her lips. In any quarrel, Sacha would remain devastatingly the master. How often she had ranted and railed at him, only to have him demolish her emotional arguments with a few taunting, cutting phrases! In the past, it had infuriated her, and gained her exactly nothing. Well, she had gone down that road too often to make the mistake of challenging him with no better weapons than her tongue and temper. So, she met his sardonic eyes calmly and nodded.

Thinking about Sacha, and the most potent weapon he used to keep her in subjection, she realised that she hadn't been entirely honest with him about the men in her life. Not that she had any intention of telling him everything he asked about her past. But she had dated other men, although it had been nothing serious, and they had been casual dates arranged for the most part, by Pat, anxious to link her up with a second husband. At the first sign of intimacy, even a kiss, Katie had broken off at once. But she had no intention of telling Sacha that, either. Pat had once asked her if she had trouble 'loosening up' with her husband, and in a roundabout way Katie knew she was asking her if she had been frigid during her marriage. Far from it! Katie had never told her the truth—that she had never found anyone who could compare with Sacha.

It was ironical, therefore, that Sacha would think she was so man-hungry that she would respond to anyone the way she reponded to him. And it gave her an idea of what the future would be like unless she asserted herself. Whatever else happened, she was determined that Sacha was not going to find her a pushover, easily mastered, subservient to his wishes, as she had been before. Easy and boring, in other words, thought Katie grimly—something she hadn't been in a long time and please God, would never be again!

'Katie, who in the world is that gorgeous man in the kitchen, feeding Kim cornflakes? Is it true that he's Kim's father?'

It was Pat, who flounced into the room in her usual uninhibited fashion. Katie took one look at her familiar face and sat down on the bed and burst into tears. Between sobs, she managed to gasp out part of her story, or at least enough to give Pat an idea of what had happened. Until now Pat had assumed, like everyone else, that Katie was a widow, and she could feel Pat's shock from where she sat. But she loyally remained at her friend's side, rubbing Katie's shoulder and handing her tissues between clucks of sympathy.

'But, Katie,' she said at last, hesitantly, 'I don't know what the problem is, sweetie. Most women would give ten years of their lives to have a man like that—rich, handsome, famous, and wanting you to come back to him. Oh, yes, I understand that he asked you for a divorce,' she interrupted herself hastily, 'but so what? You have a baby now, and that's all past history. Try to forgive and forget as he has. Unless,' she added, with a trace of embarrassment, 'Katie, is it—your old trouble? Does he—er—turn you off?'

Katie laughed a little wildly. 'Far from it! All he has to do is touch me and I'm on fire! In fact, he doesn't even have to do anything but look at me for me to——' She stopped, biting her lip, too humiliated to complete her confession.

'For you to want him?' Pat asked gently. 'Okay, honey, I understand now. And I understand something else, too— why none of the men I introduced you to ever made the grade with you. But, Katie, is that wrong? To want your own husband?'

'But I don't want to be like I was before,' Katie said desperately. 'I don't want to lose all my self-respect. Oh, Pat, you don't know! I was such a silly little fool then. I— he was my teacher, you see, at the Art Institute. He was eleven years older than I was and a perfect dreamboat— and already a famous artist. He didn't need the money, but they persuaded him to take just one class. It meant a lot to the school just to have his name on the faculty list. I used to hang around outside just to watch him leave, or turn up looking for a table in the school cafeteria while he was having coffee. Oh, I was so transparent!' she added ironically. 'Finally, he asked me for a date—well, why not? I practically threw myself at him. He must have thought I was an experienced little nympho, but during the course of the evening he made the obvious discovery from my reactions that I was a virgin. I was only eighteen and had just lost my father and had never really known my mother, and—and I was all alone in the world and—I ended up sitting on his lap, bawling my eyes out. I think he must have been appalled and amused, too, but he certainly wasn't in love with me! However, he apparently felt responsible for me after that, because he told me—not asked me!—that we were getting married. Oh, I was a spineless little fool.'

'But you're not spineless now, Katie,' Pat reassured her stoutly. 'At least, I don't think you are. You're the strongest person I know. Look how you took hold after your Aunt Anna died. You hadn't a cent and you had a baby to support, yet you turned this place into something worthwhile singlehanded. And all from nothing!'

'I hope you're right—about me, Pat, because I'm going to need every bit of the strength I have. Sacha isn't going to be satisfied with anything less than total capitulation.'

'Is that what he wants of you?' Pat asked curiously. 'Is that what went wrong the last time?'

'Oh, no, I'd probably still be clinging like a helpless little barnacle if he hadn't kicked me out,' Katie replied drearily. 'I knew what the score was, of course. He didn't love me, but for a while it was enough just to love him and know that I was his wife. But finally I got greedy—I started wanting more. I wanted him to love me. I had a friend—Irene West—who wanted my husband, only I hadn't the sense to see it. She convinced me that he was cheating on me and prodded me into throwing scenes and making accusations. Sacha got irritated—and bored—and when Sacha was bored, he showed it, which made me worse. Finally he asked me for a divorce.'

'I think he may be surprised this time around.' Pat grinned. 'You've grown up, honey. You're *not* boring and you can pack an awful wallop of your own if anyone starts pushing you around. And how!' The grin widened. 'Now! One of your troubles is over. I want to buy this place if you're serious about selling it. I've been thinking of asking you about a partnership for some time now that Trish will be going to school in the fall, and I'll need something to keep me busy.'

Katie was overwhelmed with relief. Although details had to be worked out—she to come to a fair price and Pat to 'hit her ex-husband for a loan', as she put it—she could relax now that her hard-won little shop was not going to fall into unappreciative hands. 'And if you ever decide *you're* bored and want to come back,' Pat promised, 'then I'll sell you a half interest back.'

But Katie knew she would not be coming back. She had not told Pat about Sacha's ultimatum, but so long as he held that over her head she knew that she had to make this marriage work, no matter how much humiliation she had to suffer in the process.

Back in the kitchen, Pat told Sacha the news, flirting with him the way she did with most men. Katie watched tolerantly. Once, Pat's smiles and blushes would have set her on fire with jealousy, not to mention that gleam in Sacha's eyes as he watched her, but she had come a long way since then. It was Katie who insisted on Pat staying and having a drink to celebrate the sale. She unearthed a half-empty bottle of sherry in the cupboard and divided it among three coffee mugs, and Sacha, propped against the old rolltop desk, toasted the new management.

'Who made those framed collages in the nursery, Katie?' he asked idly.

'Katie did,' Pat bubbled. 'She's a talented gal! Give her a few scraps of cloth and an embroidery needle and she can turn out a picture, or a wall hanging or—or a patchwork skirt! But then you know that—you were her teacher.'

'I'm afraid I don't know that,' he replied smoothly. 'Of course, as her teacher, I knew Katie couldn't paint. Sometimes I wondered what she was doing in my class.' His eyes gleamed with mockery. He had *known* why she was in his class, Katie thought sickly, squirming at the memory of her lovesick idolatry. 'But I'm glad to hear that she has unsuspected talents. The collages are very good. I just hope I can provide her with enough scope when she begins decorating our home.'

Katie was stunned by the unexpected compliment, but Pat was unflappable. 'Oh, she'll do a marvellous job!' she enthused. 'She has a flair for colour and design. In fact, you're lucky all around, because Katie is also a super cook.'

Sacha looked amused. 'Really?'

Katie kicked Pat under the table, stopping her in mid-phrase. 'Isn't it time we were going?' she asked pointedly.

'Of course. I'm afraid I forgot the time—the conversation was so interesting,' Sacha added wickedly. 'I'd love to hear more about Katie another time, Pat, but we have a long trip ahead of us and two very anxious people at the end of it.'

'They know we're coming, then?'

'Yes, I called my father while you were packing. He's very excited at the prospect of seeing his grandson.'

CHAPTER FOUR

Just walk away and try to forget the shop ever existed.'
Pat was dangling Katie's keys from her fingers and hanging
over the car window, bright-eyed with excitement.

'We're trying to,' Sacha murmured under his breath,
but his voice held an undertone of laughter, as though he
found Pat's bubbling enthusiasm amusing.

The suitcases had been loaded into the car; Kim and
Sammy were in as well as Katie, but Pat was still talking.

'I promise I won't call on her for a single thing, not even
if there's an emergency,' she said to Sacha.

'May we count on that?' he asked ironically.

He sat beside Katie, his hands resting loosely on the
wheel, watching narrow-eyed as he listened to Pat. He was
cool and in control, not giving anything away by so much
as an inch, thought Katie. As she huddled in one corner of
the front seat and held a sleepy Kim in her arms, she
wondered if his veins held ice water. It was always that
way—from the beginning Sacha had never lost his head
whereas she had always been an emotional little fool, easily
led, easily swayed. Suddenly, she felt absolutely certain
that she had let herself in for an outsized dose of heart-
break.

She stirred restlessly, and as though he had read her
mind, Sacha cut Pat off with a quick, crisp goodbye, and
backed the Mercedes out of the driveway.

Katie had no idea where they were going, and found it
almost too easy to leave it in Sacha's hands, but when she
saw the helicopter awaiting them at the airstrip, she was
shaken sharply out of her apathy.

It was red and blue, and across the door was a dashing inscription, 'Kimberly Ranch.' Sacha's impatient hand at her back forced her forward, reminding her to control her fears about flying before Kim. As she was being buckled into her seat belt and given Sammy to hold, she was attacked by an irrational panic. She had flown once—to Hawaii—but that was in a large jet, which gave one the illusion of being in a train. But this was different, with the blades clacking overhead, and the earth rapidly drooping away beneath one's feet. She could hear Kim's excited voice as he was lifted into the seat behind her, and then, to her unspeakable horror, she saw that Saccha was calmly climbing into the pilot's seat and was strapping himself into his belt.

She drew in a sharp, terrified breath.

'You—you don't mean you're going to d-drive this thing!' she stammered.

He glanced at her sharply. 'I've been a licensed pilot since I was eighteen,' he said dryly. 'My father was too busy to depend upon commercial aircraft, and he pressed me into service.' He seemed unaware of her nervousness as he put on a very efficient set of earphones.

The giant whirlybird rose smoothly, hovered and began a southward course, and Katie gave herself over to trying to quell her nervous fears and quiet her equally nervous stomach.

Sacha glanced at her once or twice, but he said nothing until the aircraft tilted, and he pointed out that they were coming in to Hawaii. Katie looked down cautiously. In the light of the setting sun, Hawaii glowed like an emerald set in a field of iridescent colours, mostly a range of blues shot through with gold, green and an occasional flash of red. Katie had never been here, since the infrequent vacations she allowed herself had, of necessity, to be spent on Oahu. She knew little about it, except as the largest of the

group of islands that made up the state of Hawaii, and
that it was considered by many people to be the most
beautiful, with its rising cliffs, silvery waterfalls and a vol-
cano that brought thousands of tourists each year to stand
at its edge and gape. She saw none of that, but gained a
fleeting impression of green fields, roads, a sparse settle-
ment or two, and then the airstrip. The helicopter hovered
like an awkward, ungainly, noisy bird, then slowly it began
to descend, but Katie did not relax until it finally bumped
gently to the ground.

This time their car was a battered station wagon. It was
driven out from a heavily padlocked garage as soon as the
helicopter blades came to a stop. Sacha swung the suitcases
into the back, then stood talking in a low voice to the
uniformed guard who had driven the car on to the field.

Meantime, Katie settled into the car with Sammy and
Kim. Kim crawled into her lap, his thumb in his mouth,
just as Sacha opened the door on the driver's side.

'I'm sleepy, Mummy.'

'I'm not surprised,' she said tartly.

'Don't let him get too comfortable. We haven't far to
go.' By the reflected light from the dashboard, Katie saw
he was frowning as he leaned forward to turn on the ignition.

'What's the matter?' she asked.

'Probably nothing, but Frank said that a stranger has
been hanging around the airfield, asking questions.'

'A stranger?'

'We try to be careful, discreet,' he explained quietly.
'This car, for instance; an electronic fence; alarms, guard
dogs; but inevitably, a rich man's family is a target for—
er—cranks.'

'Are you talking about *kidnappers*?' Katie gasped.

He shrugged. 'Perhaps.' His voice was carefully emo-
tionless.

She clutched Kim closer. 'B-b-but p-people don't know—— Would they have learned already about Kim? There was only that one time in the paper that your mother was mentioned——' she begged.

'No,' he agreed gently. 'Kim isn't in danger of kidnappers because of my mother, but because of my father.'

'Your father? You said he was a rancher!'

A fleeting look of amusement crossed his face. 'He's also a rich man. Oh, don't worry, we have good protection,' he added roughly. 'The estate is well guarded and the men he employs are loyal.'

By this time they had arrived at a pair of forbidding gates set in a heavy steel fence, half hidden by shrubbery. The gates opened smoothly to the touch of an electronic switch in the car. The headlights briefly picked up the outline of a dark, tree-lined drive before the car was swallowed up in the blackness of a tropical undergrowth on either side. The drive lasted about half a mile before the strong beams illuminated an inner gate guarded by a pair of stone rams and they entered a courtyard paved with crushed stone. Katie saw the outline of a house, a large, impressive-looking place with a recessed second floor surrounded by a balcony.

As the car came to a stop, outside lights sprang up, the front door was thrown open and an elderly Japanese manservant in a white jacket hurried down the steps.

'Welcome, welcome, Mr Sacha.' He was beaming. 'Your father awaits you. Most anxious to see the little one.'

'Thank you, Yoshura,' Sacha replied easily. 'This is Mrs Kimberly and this little sleepyhead is Kim,' he added, lifting the boy carefully from Katie's lap.

Yoshura bowed smilingly, then busied himself with removing the luggage from the car. Sacha led the way into the house, carrrying Kim, and Katie trailed behind uncertainly. By this time she was feeling extremely apprehensive, her stomach was fluttering with nervousness and her mouth was dry. She knew that part of her problem was hunger, but her feelings were not helped when she saw the rich interior of the house.

Sacha led the way into the living room and Katie followed. Her first confused impression was of spaciousness and light, of muted furniture and carpets accented by the glowing colours of an antique Chinese screen, Oriental paintings and a priceless collection of porcelain in a lacquer cabinet. She moved timidly closer to Sacha, then she was meeting Sacha's father.

Paul Kimberly was shorter than his son, with swarthier skin, but they had the same dark eyes and thin-lipped mouth. The thick black hair, in the father's case, was liberally streaked with grey. He was dressed casually and comfortably in a loose-fitting tunic that was tied at the waist by a sash and was worn over a pair of loose cotton slacks. On his feet were thonged sandals.

He greeted her warmly. 'At last I meet you, daughter-in-law! I bid you welcome to my house, Katie.'

'Thank you, Mr Kimberly.' Katie took his outstretched hand.

'Please, don't call me that. If you can't bring yourself to call me Father, then you may call me Paul,' he commanded smilingly, but his eyes had already turned to his grandson. Sacha had put the little boy on his feet, but Kim was clinging to his leg. An oddly moved look crossed the older man's face and he drew a deep breath. 'Ah-h-h! He looks exactly like you, Sacha. A mirror image! Thank God there'll be no awkward questions asked now.'

'He's my son, Father. I wouldn't expect anyone to ask me questions,' Sacha said grimly.

'Yes, yes, I know. But you can't halt gossip, my son,' his father reminded him impatiently.

'Is that why my grandmother isn't here?' Sacha

demanded. 'Because she thinks the child isn't mine?'

His father looked slightly embarrassed. 'She's—old,' he murmured. 'Give her time to come around.'

Sacha knelt and disengaged the little boy's clinging fingers, then whispered something in his ear. Solemnly Kim walked over to his grandfather and tugged at his hand. When the old man bent down he planted a moist kiss on the lined cheek.

'He's—wonderful, Sacha.' There was a slight break in his voice. 'Thank you for bringing my grandson to me.'

Sacha's hands curved possessively around the small waist. 'Yes,' he said deeply. 'Katie has borne a nice child.'

'Er—yes, of course.' Obviously Paul Kimberly had forgotten all about her. 'A fine boy, Katie.'

Katie, who had been feeling almost like an Indian squaw delegated to await her master's pleasure in the back of the tent, wondered wryly how much credit he really gave her in producing Kim.

'Bless my soul! What's that—thing?' Suddenly, Paul had noticed Sammy, who was hovering anxiously at Katie's feet, his worried little face indicating all too plainly that he considered himself to be lost.

Sacha's rueful eyes met Katie's. 'Sorry, Father, but that's—er—Sammy. And where Kim goes, he goes, too. He's housebroken and we'll try to keep him off the furniture, but you know how it is with a boy and his dog.'

'Of course, of course, son. I like a dog, but your grandmother may think his place is outside.'

'No!' Kim dropped to his knees and clutched Sammy in his arms. 'I don't want him to go outside. He's my dog!'

'No one is going to take Sammy away from you, Kim,' Sacha said gently. 'But he must eat his dinner right now. Would you let Yoshura take him to the kitchen if he promises to bring him back before you go to bed?'

Kim looked at the smiling Japanese butler, then handed Sammy reluctantly into the waiting arms.

'I have good dinner in the kitchen for little fellow, Kim,' Yoshura promised.

'Katie's dead on her feet, Father,' Sacha added. 'The sooner she and Kim go to bed, the better. Perhaps they can have a tray in their rooms?'

'Of course,' Paul replied courteously. 'You take them upstairs, Sacha—you know the way. I think your grandmother set aside the master suite with that little dressing room next door for Kim. Meantime, I'll see Yoshura about a tray.'

The first thing Katie saw in the big, luxurious bedroom was the king-size bed, covered by a rich raw silk bedspread. It was opulent, suggestive, and it seemed to her tired eyes to dominate the room. She whirled to look at Sacha, and from the wickedly amused look on his face she knew just what he was thinking. Her mouth tightened.

'I'm not sharing that bed with you, Sacha!' she hissed.

'You are, you know,' he said gently. 'Sooner than you think. However, I agree that tonight you're in no condition to fight for your virtue. Come, let me show you.' He led her through an adjoining door to another bedroom, just as luxurious but with slightly more masculine furnishings. 'This is where I'll be sleeping.'

On the other side of her bedroom was a dressing room about the size of her bedroom back in the bungalow. It was fitted with wall-to-wall, ceiling-to-floor closets, more space than she could ever imagine needing. A cot had been set up, and a small chest of drawers had been hastily shoved into a space by the window. Through an adjoining open door Katie glimpsed the fixtures of a bathroom.

'I'm too old for a cot!' Kim's lower lip was thrust out and his mouth was trembling.'

'Of course you are,' Sacha agreed cheerfully. 'We'll get

rid of it first thing tomorrow.'

Kim brightened. 'I want to sleep with Mommy!' he demanded. ''Less you are, Daddy—are you going to sleep with Mommy, Daddy? Trisha says daddies and mommies sleep together.'

'They do in the best families,' Sacha said solemnly. 'What about it, Mommy?'

'Little pitchers have big ears,' Katie replied blandly, swooping down and lifting Kim into the cot. 'If you don't sleep here, what's Sammy going to do? He won't have anyone to sleep with.'

Presented with that argument Kim stuck his thumb into his mouth as he considered. 'I'll sleep in the cot—just for tonight,' he agreed, briefly releasing his thumb.

Just then a discreet knock heralded the entrance of Yoshura, with a covered tray. Sammy trotted beside him, and it was obvious that he had been fed from the way his small pink tongue was busily licking his mouth. He thoroughly investigated his new home, then settled down with a sigh beneath Kim's cot. While Katie was hunting for Kim's duck and bear, there was a dead silence from the dressing room, and when she went in with his tray it was to find Kim asleep and Sammy stretched out full length, his head on his paws.

'He's asleep?' Sacha murmured, just behind her.

'Yes.'

'It would be much easier,' Sacha mused, as they came out and shut the door behind them, 'if we began tonight as we mean to go on. I could share that supper with you, and then the bed——'

'No!' she cried stormily, and a flush coloured her cheeks and throat.

'We did make a bargain, you know,' he said thoughtfully.

'You'll have to wait!' She swallowed convulsively. 'I'm

not ready to—to become a wife again. After all, it's been five years——'

'But you are,' he said sardonically. 'I think I proved that today. Do you really think I couldn't have had you then, if I hadn't been the one to call a halt?'

'Very well, I'm vulnerable,' she agreed painfully. 'I admit it. And you're an expert. After all, you've had plenty of experience, and you know exactly what buttons to push to make me want you. But th-that doesn't mean I'm willing.'

'Indeed? What a little hypocrite you've become, Katie!' he said ironically. 'At least you used to be honest. Are you trying to tell me that if I'd taken you today, it would have been against your will?'

'In a—way.' Her cheeks reddened as she met his eyes.

'And what's the magic formula?' he sneered. 'At what point do we stop calling it rape and admit that we both want to make love? Or——' his eyes glittering dangerously, his voice deepened, 'is that what you want, Katie? For me to rape you so that you can pretend it was against your will?'

She paled. 'No!'

'Don't panic. I don't intend to oblige,' he said coolly. 'I don't intend to give you an out that way. Neither will I become your whipping boy, Katie, while you try to psycho-analyse your feelings and desires.'

'It's not that.' Helplessly, she tried to explain. 'It's just that—this time—I want it to be better——'

'There was nothing wrong with our marriage the last time except that you needed to grow up,' he interrupted brutally. 'Time has taken care of that. Now you've been presented with a dilemma, which is whether to take me willingly or make a show of reluctance so as to punish me a little. I had thought you mature enough to recognise your own needs, but apparently I was mistaken.'

She hung her head, miserably conscious that she could not articulate the way she felt. A great deal had been said about needs, she thought bitterly, but they had all been of the flesh. Nothing had been mentioned about the needs of the spirit and heart, and she could not bring it up, since Sacha had not. God knows, she hadn't much pride, but she had too much to expose herself so pitilessly.

'Meantime, I'm serving notice on you, Katie. You're on borrowed time. No matter how much you wriggle and twist, we're married, and we're going to stay that way—for the boy's sake, if no other. We can't afford to indulge ourselves first. Accept it, Katie! We're yoked together from now on whether we like it or not.'

Such grim, unyielding words! They fell like a death knell on Katie's hopes of gaining Sacha's love. Was this, then, how he felt?

He waited, and when she did not reply, he strolled over to the door and flung it open. 'Goodnight,' he said savagely. 'And pleasant dreams!'

CHAPTER FIVE

'GOOD morning, Mrs Kimberly.'

Katie sat up in bed and stared at the uniformed maid, the unfamiliar greeting still ringing in her ears. The girl was very pretty, with black, almond-shaped eyes and a delicate, pearl-like complexion. She was carrying a tray that she placed on a table. 'Here is your breakfast.' She lifted silver covers from various dishes. 'Mr Sacha said to let you sleep as late as you liked, but the Old Madam said to awaken you.'

'What time is it?' asked Katie.

'Nearly ten o'clock, ma'am. The Old Madam wishes to see you in the atrium as soon as you finish breakfast.' She went over and pulled the silk curtains back with a swish, letting in warm air and sunlight. Through an open window Katie heard a child's laughter and she glanced at the closed dressing room door.

'My son—where is he?'

'He and his father were up early, ma'am. They are at the stables now, I believe. Mr Sacha said something about teaching him to ride.'

'To ride?' Katie cried sharply. 'But he can't! Kim's never been on a horse in his life! He's only a baby!' She swung her feet over the side of the bed and started to scramble hastily through the suitcase she had been too tired to unpack the night before.

'Here, let me do that.' The girl took the clothes from her hands and folded them neatly. 'He'll come to no harm, ma'am—Mr Sacha will see to that. There are some very gentle horses in the stables.' Her words were meant to be reassuring. 'Now, come over and have your breakfast.'

Katie went over to the table and sat down slowly. The fragrant odour of coffee tantalised her nostrils and her stomach gurgled protestingly. She took a tentative mouthful and discovered that she was ravenous. Last night her dinner, a chicken casserole cooked with various herbs, mushrooms and wild rice, had been delicious, as had been the accompanying salad and the light chocolate mousse that followed, but she had been too tired and tense to eat much of it. It had taken hours to fall asleep in spite of her exhaustion, and then, when she finally slipped off near dawn, she had slept as heavily as though she had been drugged. But she recognised the absurdity of becoming upset merely because Kim was at the stables. Sacha would not allow any harm to come to him. After all, wasn't that what this reconciliation was all about?

The food was good—iced melon, fresh orange juice, a fluffy omelette with bacon—and although it was more than she usually ate, she was enjoying it. 'What's your name?' she asked the girl, who was busy unpacking her case.

'Lurilana, ma'am.'

'Are you Hawaiian, or——' Katie paused, not knowing how to phrase it.

'Half and half. My father was Chinese. In other words, I am a typical Hawaiian,' the girl added, giggling.

Katie smiled. It was true—Hawaii *was* the home of a variety of people with different backgrounds, cultures, racial mixtures, all living together and mixing very well on the whole, in spite of—or perhaps because of—their differences.

'You said something about the Old Madam,' she said slowly. 'I presume you meant my husband's grandmother?'

'Yes, ma'am. Now, she is a *pure* Hawaiian!' Lurilana commented admiringly. 'She married old Mr Kimberly when there weren't too many white men living on this island. He is dead now, of course. And I have been told that she had many children, but only Mr Paul survived. He was her youngest.'

'There was a lot of infant mortality in those days,' Katie remarked absently.

'Yes, ma'am.'

She sounded imperious, Katie thought wryly. Old Madam, indeed! Last night she had refused to receive her, but this morning, she was being summoned to the Presence. Who had forced her hand? Paul—or Sacha? Katie dreaded the meeting. She looked around the room speculatively as she sipped her coffee. Everything here spoke of money, even the bathroom, which was lined with some sort of rare, fragrant Oriental wood. So why was she looking for difficulties when she could live in a house like this? But it wasn't home, and it made her sick with longing for Katie's Place.

She sighed. The problem was not where they lived but how she could live with Sacha and maintain her self-respect. Oh, she could give in and allow Sacha to drug her into forgetfullness with his sensual expertise. That was how it had happened last time. For a while, that kind of passion might even pass for love, but sooner or later even Sacha was going to long for more. He was basically a sensitive man. How long would it take him before he started seeking someone who could give him something more, something that was not merely a physical relationship? How long would he remain faithful before he turned to someone like Claire Wetherell?

And herself? How long could she exist on the edge of Sacha's life, satisfied with the crumbs?

She got up restlessly and went to the bathroom to take a shower. When she came out Lurilana had gone, leaving draped over the bed a blue polyester skirt and blouse, full-flowing and sleeveless, with a tie belt. Under the bed was a matching pair of high-heeled sandals. Apparently this was her choice for Katie to wear when meeting Old Madam, so Katie took the hint. It was a favourite dress of hers, and anyway she didn't have that many choices among her limited wardrobe.

She confined her make-up to just a touch of lipstick, a swirl of the mascara brush and a dash of a light floral scent that blended with, rather than masked, the clean, subtle fragrance of soap and water. Her long, blonde-streaked hair was clipped at the nape with a favourite slide. Leaning forward, Katie surveyed herself dissatisfiedly in the mirror. I look like a milkmaid, she thought disgustedly, even to the freckles on my nose, and a memory of Claire Wetherell's cool beauty slid unwillingly into her mind.

Downstairs she found the atrium without any difficulty. It was situated in the centre of the house and was surrounded on all sides by a covered porch, with chairs and tables placed at convenient places. There were also pots and jars of blooming plants and miniature shrubs—hibiscus, oleanders and gardenias. They had apparently just been watered, and gave off a damp, woodsy odour. The atrium itself was patterned after a Japanese garden, with strategically placed rocks and stone lanterns.

Two elderly women were seated on the porch, playing cards at one of the tables. Katie had no trouble deciding which was Madame Kimberly. Her companion was small and shrunken with a face like a withered apple. The Old Madam was in a wheelchair, and as her brown, arthritic hands dealt the cards, diamonds flashed on most of her fingers. Her coal-black hair was worn in a chignon, with a jewelled fanlike comb thrust through its knot. She was wearing a black silk muu-muu that matched the snapping black eyes that she raised at Katie's approach.

'You know who I am, of course?' she asked arrogantly, in a hoarse, cracked voice.

'Naturally,' Katie replied coolly. The old woman *was* intimidating, but Katie had no intention of allowing her to see that she was inwardly quaking.

'Sit down.' Madam Kimberly waved a clawlike hand. 'My son says I owe you an apology for not meeting you last night. Frankly, I wanted time to think about my position in this. The old, you see, are slow to accept new ideas, and it was disconcerting to learn that I had just acquired a new great-grandson.'

Does she call that an apology? Katie wondered, but she kept her face expressionless as she asked sweetly, 'And now that you've had time to think about it?'

'Now that I have met him,' Madam Kimberly went on, after giving her a sharp glance as though she suspected sarcasm, 'I know, whatever I might think about the convenience of you showing up at this time, that the child *is* Sacha's son. He is the absolute image of my dead husband, except my husband's eyes were blue. Oola agrees with me about this.'

'Oola?' queried Katie.

'My companion.'

Katie glanced at the other old woman who met her look impassively. 'I see,' she said dryly. With an effort she reminded herself that the Old Madam *was* very old and she might not be aware that she had just implied a slur on Katie's character. Thank goodness Sacha did not intend to live here for long.

'Have you been well treated? Made comfortable?' Madam Kimberly asked distantly.

'Yes, thank you,' Katie replied in an equally distant voice. 'My room is very comfortable and my breakfast this morning was delicious.'

'I am glad to hear that the servants are maintaining their usual perfect standards. It is not the custom of the family to breakfast in bed,' she added blandly, 'but we are always willing to oblige our guests.'

Another slur, or an implication that she was not one of the family! Katie's temper simmered, but she managed to avoid showing it, knowing that nothing would make the Old Madam angrier than to see her slurs miss their mark. 'Thank you,' she said politely, 'I'll remember that. And now perhaps I'd better look up Sacha and Kim. Are they still at the stables?'

'No, they're not!' Madam snapped irritably. 'Claire came over earlier and drove them to her ranch. She raises thoroughbred horses and she thought she might have a pony that would do for Kim.' A faint softening of the lined features told Katie that Madam Kimberly approved of Claire.

'I shouldn't think we would be here long enough to bother with buying a pony,' Katie remarked aloofly, and was taken aback by the old woman's instant violent reaction.

'Not be here? How dare you say that? *Sacha* will be here, impertinent Miss, and so will his son! This is his home, and you're only here on sufferance!' An angry flush mottled her face. 'So, already you want to make changes. You want to abuse my hospitality and steal my grandson—and yes, my great-grandson! I'm not surprised. It's no more than I expected, than I was told would happen. Well, I won't allow it, you hear—I won't allow it! You go away! You're not wanted here!'

Oola stood up, alarmed, and Katie reached the old woman's side at the same time. She tried to calm her. 'Please, Madam Kimberly, do not distress yourself,' she said soothingly. 'I'm not trying to take Sacha away from his home or—or steal anyone. I didn't know you felt this way about it.'

Madam glared at her. 'No,' she snapped, 'you don't know anything! You don't know about me, or Sacha either, for that matter. But why should I worry? You count for nothing in his life. He won't be influenced by a chit like you!' Oola had poured out a glass of water, and she waved it away petulantly. 'Don't fuss so. Sit down, sit down, both of you. It's time I learned something about you, girl. It's Katie, isn't it?' The shaking lips firmed with disgust. 'A foolish, ill-conceived name! Well, tell me about yourself, Katie. Do you ride, for instance?'

Katie sat down and looked at her cautiously. She had certainly changed her tune in a hurry! Had someone told her she must try to make friends with her new grand-daughter? Just the same, her outbreak had certainly been revealing. Madam Kimberly did not want her here, and Katie wondered if Paul's friendliness had covered a similar dislike. She felt dispirited; she had liked Paul.

'No, Madam, I don't ride,' she said shortly. 'My child-hood was not privileged and riding lessons were out of the question. Although we were not poor, we didn't have any money for luxuries. My mother died when I was four years old, and my father, who was an artist, was not particularly successful.'

It was a blunt, unadorned statement, and successfully glossed over the happy years of her childhood which had been spent with a gay, feckless father who managed to invest even the economies they had to practise with a sense of adventurous fun. Not for anything would she describe her foolish, impractical father to this awful old woman, she thought defiantly.

'Humph! I can see you're not from Sacha's world, if you don't even know how to ride a horse. What else will we learn about you, I wonder? You do realise, don't you, that you'll be left out of things around here unless you ride? Sacha spends a lot of time on horseback when he's here at the ranch. Now he'll be spending it all with Claire!'

Katie managed to look bored and uninterested as she

drawled, 'Really? I presume, then, that Mrs Wetherell rides very well?'

Madam Kimberly's black eyes snapped with delight. 'Yes, indeed! She carries away all the rosettes at the shows. She was Sacha's childhood sweetheart, you know. She married Wetherell when she heard that Sacha had married you and divorced him when she learned that you and Sacha were separated.' Poor Wetherell, Katie thought. 'She has bought the ranch next to this one just to be near Sacha.'

Katie wondered if she was supposed to congratulate Claire's perseverance, but she contented herself with murmuring that she seemed like a good friend. Unfortunately, Madam had no sense of humour and took it at face value.

'I wouldn't say that. They were going to be married— until yesterday, when you came back into his life.'

What a dreadful old woman! thought Katie indignantly. And what was one supposed to reply to such an outrageous remark? 'Sacha can't marry anyone else—he's already married to me,' she said stiffly.

'A mistake that can be corrected,' Madam assured her smoothly. 'Sacha will gain a great deal if—when—he marries Claire. She is another *kamaaina*, she loves Hawaii, and will always want to live here, and also, he will have an important sponsor in Claire's father, who is a famous collector and connoisseur of modern art.'

'Indeed?' Katie's hands were shaking, but she managed to hide them in the folds of her skirt. 'Are you implying that I should step aside for Claire Wetherell, Madam Kimberly?'

'I would not presume to meddle between you and your husband, my dear girl,' Madam said silkily. 'I am merely trying to acquaint you with the plans that were afoot until yesterday.'

'I didn't *force* Sacha to take me back——'

'How, otherwise, would he get his son?' Madam demanded.

Shocked, Katie realised that she had forgotten Kim temporarily. Of course, that was why the reconciliation—hadn't Sacha himself told her so? 'Sacha may have a divorce if he likes——' she began stiffly.

'Yes, I know,' Madam purred hoarsely. 'As soon as he heard about the child yesterday, my son Paul called his lawyers. They have assured him that Sacha has a good case to gain complete custody of the child. I am not sure if he will agree, however. He has—pity for you.'

'Pity? For me?' Katie leaped to her feet, humiliated and outraged. Had Sacha been discussing her with this evil old woman? 'He needn't pity *me*!' she said indignantly. 'If he wants a divorce, he can have one, and it won't cost him a cent! But just let him try taking Kim away from me, and I'll fight! Just let him try!'

She turned and ran out of the atrium, the memory of Madam Kimberly's triumphant look following her. Inside, she hesitated. The faint humming of the vacuum cleaner and far-off voices told her that the servants were busy upstairs. Where could she go? She wanted to run back to Honolulu, to the mainland, but she knew that running away was no answer now. Even if she succeeded, she couldn't hope to hide from Sacha, and this time he would have the full resources of the law backing him.

No—better play it cool, remain calm. Madam Kimberly was a pinprick. Her fate depended upon Sacha, and he wanted her, not a divorce. Even though it was on Kim's account, there was something comforting about knowing she was valued for some reason. After all, she told herself bravely, although he might want Claire for a wife, it was she who was Kim's mother, and that made her position invulnerable. She must keep telling herself that, and she would be all right. And hadn't the old Madam perhaps needled her deliberately in the hope that she would hysterically demand that Sacha give her a divorce? Yes, the more Katie thought about the recent scene, the more pat it seemed. The old woman was clever, and it would suit her immensely to have Katie throw a scene while she wore the bewildered look of innocence.

Meantime, Katie desperately needed a breathing space, and she could not get it in here, where at any moment Madam Kimberly might decide to wheel herself through that door—— With a shudder, Katie dashed out of the room, through another, and out of a door that opened upon a patio and outside.

A row of distant rooftops made her think that this might be the way to the stables. She cut through some shrubbery and followed a well worn path to what was indeed the stables, very trim and smart, encircled by a fenced pasture. A tractor stood idle at the end of a sweep of gravelled driveway. There were no ranch hands about, but Kim was hanging on to the fence, gazing raptly at some horses frisking in the pasture. And of course there was Sammy, stretched out, waiting, his tongue lolling as he watched his little master.

A little red sports car—Katie had no idea of its make or model—was in the driveway and beside it, lost in a world of their own, were Sacha and Claire Wetherell. Katie recognised her instantly and, with a sinking feeling, saw that she was as beautiful as she remembered.

Claire was doing all the talking. Sacha was propped against the car hood, his arms crossed and a slightly amused smile playing about his lips as he listened to her. Every word or two, as though to emphasize a point, Claire would place a proprietorial hand on Sacha's arm or touch him in some way. Once she reached up and caressingly brushed his cheek.

She was dressed in riding boots and jodhpurs. Her shirt and the scarf knotted loosely about her throat were bright yellow, a colour that contrasted vividly with her brunette beauty. Sacha, on the other hand, looked achingly familiar to Katie in a pair of faded denim jeans that fitted him like a second skin. With them he wore a short-sleeved red shirt that gaped open slightly at the neck, revealing a strong brown column of throat blurred by the hint of shadowy darkness at its base.

Sammy saw her first and hurled himself at her, barking furiously. Then Kim flung his little body into her arms, shouting, 'Mommy! Mommy! Guess what!' Katie bent over and kissed the damp, rumpled hair. 'You should see my horse! Claire says she's been saving it for a little boy just like me! He's brown with a white star on his forehead, and Daddy says I can have him you say it's all right! Please, Mommy, it is all right, isn't it?' The dark eyes were suddenly, heartbreakingly uncertain.

Katie felt a rush of gratitude to Sacha. She had not expected such consideration from him, especially after what had occurred last night and she looked up gratefully, to find him watching her oddly.

'Did you have a good rest?' he asked.

'Umm.'

He put out a careless arm and pulled her to him. He smelled warm and horsey, mixed with the strong odour of perspiring male flesh. An overwhelming wave of sensuality swept over Katie, and she buried her face weakly in his shoulder. His arm tightened.

'Come on, now, you two—no canoodling!' Claire's voice was gay—very gay, and lightly amused. 'I know you!' she added, as though she had just made a delighted discovery. 'You sold me that marvellous patchwork skirt! Remember, Sacha? I wore it to the Country Club dance.'

'And very beautiful you looked in it, too,' Sacha drawled.

Kim broke in impatiently, 'Can I, Mommy? Please say I can!'

Claire leaned over and ruffled his hair. 'Of course you can, ducky! Your mommy wouldn't think of disappointing you, would she?' She glanced ruefully at Katie. 'Better say yes, Katie. I'm afraid I ruined any chance you have of getting away with a "no". Incidentally, I adore this little son of yours. But not your dog.' With a booted foot she indicated Sammy, who backed away, showing his teeth. 'Your dog and I don't take to one another, but if you don't watch out, I'll steal your son.'

Katie looked up quickly and caught a flash of pure malice in her eyes, before the lids dropped, and Claire smiled sweetly at her.

'If you can,' Katie said gently.

'Oh, oh, the girl has issued a challenge!' Claire crowed delightedly. 'That was a mistake, wasn't it, Sacha? You know I can't resist a dare.'

'Don't be a menace, darling,' he said affectionately.

'A menace, am I?' She cocked her head pertly. 'I'd rather be alluring!'

'Surely you aren't fishing for compliments, Claire?' he asked quizzically. 'You know you're beautiful.'

'But you've never painted me,' she pouted. 'Are you afraid you won't be able to get the real me on canvas?'

'You haven't a paintable face,' he said dryly. 'You're not like Katie, for instance.'

'Oh, now I know what you mean by a paintable face! No, thank you, I'd rather be beautiful and alluring!'

The words sounded to Katie like an insult, but Sacha only grinned and said indulgently, 'Don't be a brat. Behave yourself! I like to paint Katie because her face is a painter's delight—it shows every mood.'

'In other words, she's predictable and lacks mystery?' Claire said innocently.

The whole exchange had become a sparring match between Sacha and Claire. Katie thought Claire was rather like a soft little kitten, trying out her claws in the hide of a large, deceptively lazy lion. The scratches that the little kitten inflicted were mere pinpricks; the real claws were for Katie.

'Mommy's face gets real red when she's mad,' Kim said thoughtfully, and Sacha burst out laughing.

'Stop teasing your mommy,' Claire scolded him softly. 'She can't help her face. It's not kind of you two!' She turned to Katie, the warm smile she was wearing not quite hiding the malicious glitter of her eyes. 'I've been telling Sacha I want to give you two people a party. All of Sacha's old friends will want to meet his wife, and of course, your friends will be anxious to meet Sacha. What night will suit you? A week from Friday?'

Katie looked hesitantly at Sacha. He was watching her expressionlessly. She wanted desperately to refuse, but there was no way she could phrase it without sounding impossibly churlish and ungracious. She hoped he would take it out of her hands and refuse for her, but he wasn't saying a thing.

'It—is it all right with you, Sacha?'

He regarded her thoughtfully. 'It's a good way to meet people—make friends. You'll be rather lonely if you don't.'

'I suppose so,' she muttered. 'What sort of party will it be?' she asked Claire.

'What sort would you like?' Clare asked ironically.

Katie flushed. 'I was thinking about clothes,' she said awkwardly. 'I—I didn't bring many things with me.'

Laughingly, Sacha took Kim's hand. 'Come on, son. If your mom is going to talk clothes, it's time we disappeared.'

'Don't go!' But Sacha ignored Claire's wail, and she

watched his retreating back with a hungry look that she did not bother to hide from Katie. Finally she turned back to her impatiently.

'What sort of party?' she echoed blankly. 'Oh, something simple, small and outdoorsey—around the pool. Any old thing will do. I'm going to wear a black jumpsuit myself. Why don't you run up something clever on your sewing machine, darling?' she added spitefully.

'I might, at that,' Katie replied evenly.

Claire laughed, not even bothering to disguise her contempt. 'I'm glad to have the opportunity to reach an understanding with you,' she said venomously. 'I'm sure you've been told by his grandmother that Sacha and I had planned to be married when you appeared on the scene. What she doesn't know is that we've been lovers—a long time, and will continue to be, no matter what sort of arrangement he's made to pacify you. Nothing has changed about our marriage plans, either. They've merely been temporarily postponed until Sacha gets the business of Kim straightened out.'

'There's nothing to straighten out,' Katie said sharply. 'Kim is mine.' She felt sickened by what she had heard, and she knew that her face must have paled by the triumphant look on Claire's face.

'And Sacha's,' Claire reminded her smoothly. 'I'm sure that Sacha explained to you about his determination that no child of his was going to be raised as he was—in a divided home. Therefore any woman he eventually marries will have to show that she can be a mother to Kim.'

'Kim's mine!' Katie repeated desperately.

'I've already made a good start,' Claire added. 'It will be just a matter of time before I win him over.'

'I won't give him up!' Katie felt as though she was beating her head against a stone wall. Claire was only listening to herself.

'You see,' Claire added thoughtfully, 'I've always been given everything I want. And I'm ruthless. Now, I don't even have to know you well to know you're soft as butter!' She contemplated Katie with half-closed eyes. 'One of these days you'll see for yourself that you're tearing Sacha apart by hanging on to him, not to mention Kim, and you'll get out of the picture altogether. I can do it, you see, because I have Madam Kimberly on my side. We both want the same thing—Sacha married to me, and living here in Hawaii. So think about it, my sweet, and consider if you wouldn't be wise just to get out now, before you get hurt any more than you are already.'

Madam Kimberly did not appear for lunch. Katie wondered if it was merely an instance of strategy on her part, but as time passed and no one mentioned their quarrel, she realised that Madam had told no one about it. Doubtless she was hoping that by keeping quiet, Katie would trap herself by mentioning it first, but Katie had no intention of obliging her.

As it was, she was having a hard time trying to put out of her mind what she had been told by Madam Kimberly and Claire. She reminded herself that she would be foolish to believe them. Hadn't she once believed everything Irene West had told her, hadn't it subsequently wrecked her marriage? And hadn't Sacha reminded her that she needed to grow up? But these women, his grandmother and Claire, knew him better than Irene West did, better even than Katie knew him. Wouldn't they know the truth about how he felt? She could argue that Claire might lie, because she had an axe to grind, but his grandmother loved him, she wanted him to be happy, and she had said that he loved Claire. Of course, Claire had gone beyond that and involved Kim, too, but hadn't that also had a ring of truth? And Katie had always known that a man like Sacha, imaginative, sensitive—an artist—would some day fall in love. It was just, Katie told herself wistfully, that she wished it wasn't Claire. She wasn't worthy of him. Not even for Kim's sake could she like her. Although, she reminded herself, if the divorce had gone through, Sacha would have already married Claire. There might even have been other children. Katie was surprised at the unbearable ache that thought gave her—the thought of Sacha's other children, mothered by another woman.

As lunch progressed, Katie sat quietly listening to Sacha and his father. Kim, propped up by the addition of two thick books in his chair, was not having much to say, either. Katie was not aware of the wistful quality of her stillness, nor how often both men looked at her. Paul, especially, watched her thoughtfully. Suddenly Claire's name was mentioned, piercing her indifference, and the conversation took on an intensely interesting note.

Paul mentioned that his mother had invited Claire and her father to dinner that night as their guests, and Katie, listening closely, learned from the dryly ironical way Paul said his name and Sacha's reply that neither man liked Claire's father. Apparently Mr Thorpe did not live in Hawaii, but was visiting his daughter from the mainland. Whether Claire's mother was dead or divorced, her father had been married a couple of times since. Nothing was said about the famous art collection that Madam Kimberly had mentioned, but there was a sarcastic reference to the press coverage that had been given Mr Thorpe's affairs with beautiful, well-known women. And Katie gathered that there was a tendency on the part of the women to cling, long after he had tired of them.

'Claire's thankful that he didn't bring his current mistress with him and expect her to receive the woman.' Katie thought sadly that Sacha must love Claire, to become so indignant on her behalf.

'Oh, I don't think he'd do that,' Paul said mildly. 'Ben may be a cold-hearted devil, but he's never shown disrespect to his womenfolk. Claire couldn't have seriously thought he would insult her.'

Katie, listening thoughtfully, wondered about the difference between father and son. No one could accuse Paul of being weak, yet he *was* gentle and kindly, unlike Sacha, who was apt to show his anger violently, even savagely. And Paul was master in his own home, too, in spite of his mother's strong personality. One occasionally glimpsed a hint of iron beneath that deceptively mild manner, but on the whole he must have been easy to live with. She wondered idly what had caused his marriage to fail. From the hint of sensuality in his face, she suspected that he had not been without feminine companionship all these years, but he had never put another woman in Marjorie's place. Did it mean that he still loved his ex-wife?

'What's the matter?' Sacha asked unexpectedly. 'Don't you like your lunch?'

Katie jumped. He was speaking to Kim, but she had a feeling that he was exasperated with her, too, no doubt as a carry-over from his anger with Claire's father. As a matter of fact, she did *not* like her lunch, which was an Italian dish that was too rich and highly spiced. With it they were drinking a light wine that was delicious, and under ordinary circumstances it would have been a meal that was fit for the gods, for the cooking was superb. But Katie wondered who had chosen the menu, for the meal was too heavy for such a warm day, particularly when there was to be a dinner party that night. It might do for Sacha and Paul, out all morning on horseback, but it was too much for her and Kim.

'It's too runny.' Kim's mouth drooped.

'He doesn't like spicy food,' Katie explained hastily.

'I hate it,' Kim added peevishly, for good measure.

Sacha's face darkened. 'I have no patience with food faddists. You'll learn to eat whatever's put before you, young man—the same as everyone else. The cook doesn't have time to cater to your individual taste, as apparently your mother has been in the habit of doing!'

Kim's mouth trembled, but before Katie could fly to his and her defence, Paul broke in hastily, 'Kim, if you like, I'll send one of the ranch hands over to the Wetherell place after lunch to pick up your pony.'

Kim's face lit up. 'Can I start riding lessons tomorrow?'

'I don't see why not. But you'll have to get on with your lunch, because the rest of us are waiting for you.'

'Oh, all right, Grandfather.' Kim began to eat briskly, his face wearing a dreamy smile.

'Looks like I have a lot to learn,' Sacha grinned ruefully.

'I'm afraid he's got a little spoiled.' Katie made her own apology. 'Although the food is rather rich for a child— although very good,' she added scrupulously.

'Of course it is—much too rich. For all of us. But I don't see anything amiss with speaking to the cook about preparing Kim's meals separately,' Paul added briskly. 'As for his being spoiled, I disagree. You've done a good job of raising him all by yourself, Katie. Don't blame yourself for his little quirks. On the whole, he's a good child.'

It was generous praise and went a long way towards helping Katie forget his mother's cruelty that morning. In spite of herself she felt warmed. As they were rising from the table, Paul harked back to the subject of the horse.

'How about you, Sacha? Do you want to go with Tom to get the pony? And take Kim?'

'Thanks, Father,' Sacha drawled lazily, 'but Kim's due for a nap. I think Tom can be trusted to make the pickup alone. I have something else planned with Kim this afternoon.'

'Suit yourself,' Paul shrugged, apparently unaware that

Katie had been holding her breath, wondering if Sacha would use this opportunity to see Claire again.

Which meant, Katie thought, carefully letting out her breath, that his 'something else' with Kim came before Claire, but then she knew that anyway. Even Claire admitted that Kim came first with Sacha.

Katie put Kim down for his nap in a new bed that had been hastily erected in place of the cot, then slipped on her bikini with a matching terry cloth jacket. She was headed for the pool. She had discovered it that morning while she was doing a tour of the grounds, and had been struck by its natural look, which had, of course, been carefully created by a first-class garden designer. It blended in so well with its surroundings that at first glance it looked like a rock-bound tropical pool that had been trapped in a lush undergrowth of ferns and flowers. Then one noticed the careful pruning and trimming, the natural tiled sides simulated to resemble the banks of a pool, the cleverly concealed lighting hidden under rocks and plants.

There was plenty of wooden furniture about, and Katie pulled one of the loungers into the sun, then slipped out of her coat and sank upon the cushions. With her sunglasses settled firmly on her nose, she picked up her paperback, but she didn't get beyond the first page before the sun and the heavy meal did their work. The book slid off her lap and she fell asleep.

She was awakened by the sound of Kim's voice. It sounded shrill and frightened.

'I don't want to, Daddy!'

Katie sat up with a start, and looked around. Kim and Sacha were approaching the pool. Both were dressed for swimming in shorts, and were barefoot. Sacha must have rooted through Kim's things to find his, which were last year's, and too small for him. Sacha's shorts were a pair of cut-off blue jeans, that began below the navel and left the hairy expanse of his chest and the lean, powerful legs bare. He looked big and overwhelmingly masculine, especially when compared to the small figure of his son beside him.

Katie stared, then looked away quickly but not before she registered the fact that Kim was hanging back, pulling on his father's hand, and eyeing the pool apprehensively. She drew in a dismayed breath, wondering how she could stop it.

'What are you going to do?'

Sacha was obviously surprised to see her. 'I'm going to teach him to swim,' he said evenly. 'And this is Lesson Number One.' He dropped his towel, then left Kim to wait while he slid into the pool. A couple of strokes, and he was back beside him. 'Come on, son.' He held up his arms.

'It's—too cold today.' Katie put down her book and swung her legs around to stand up. She was uncertain about the wisdom of making an active protest, especially when she saw Sacha throw her an impatient look.

'Don't be ridiculous!' he snapped. 'The pool is kept at an even temperature all year round. Besides, the sun is hot. Come on, Kim, take my hands.'

'Mommy?' Kim looked appealingly over his shoulder.

Katie rose. 'Sacha—wait. Don't you think he's a little young to be taught to swim?' With an effort she kept her voice low and controlled.

'Are you serious?' Sacha stared. 'What are you trying to do, anyway? Make him nervous of the water?'

'N-n-no, but——'

'Then shut up, unless you have something constructive to say.' By this time Kim had taken Sacha's outstretched hand, and had been pulled reluctantly into the water. He was clinging desprately to his father's neck.

'The first thing we're going to do is get you used to getting your face wet,' Sacha explained in a gentle, soothing voice. 'It's very simple. See?'

Kim lowered his face gingerly and came up gasping. 'No! No! I don't want to! Mommy! Mommy!'

Katie had abandoned all attempts to be casual and was now standing at the edge of the pool, frankly wringing her hands. 'Sacha, I know you think you're doing the best thing, but the child is frightened to death. You can't——'

He glared menacingly at her. 'All you're accomplishing is his terror. If you would stop dithering and offer some encouragement, he would stop being frightened. Suppose you get in and show him you're not afraid?'

'No, I——'

'How about it, Kim?' He placed the child on the side of the pool, and smiled mischievously at him. 'Mommy's going to come in and swim for you. She'll show you there's nothing to be afraid of.'

Kim laughed. 'Is Mommy really going to swim?'

'Of course she is—or else! Coming, Mommy?' Sacha jeered, his mocking eyes following an upward path along the trail of the brief bikini that revealed more than it covered. His eyes swelled appraisingly on the flaring hips and full breasts. 'Good thing we're secluded, darling,' he drawled lazily. 'You'd be arrested for indecent exposure if you wore that thing on the beach. Motherhood has certainly broadened your figure.'

Katie reddened and fumbled nervously with the gaping neckline of her bra. 'Sacha, please!' she mumbled embarrassedly.

'Well, what are you waiting for?' he asked crisply. 'Come on in.'

'I—I can't, Sacha. I can't—swim. I never learned how.'

His eyes widened in astonishment. '*What?*' You mean the object of all that panic was because you're afraid of the water yourself?'

'Well, I—yes.'

'What the hell was your father doing to allow you to grow up without learning to swim?' he demanded angrily.

'I doubt if he ever knew it,' Katie murmured uneasily. 'He—he just never bothered with me.'

Sacha swore, briefly and violently. Katie felt inadequate—lacking. It was almost like having a social disease, this shameful secret she had kept to herself for so long. *Everyone* was supposed to know how to swim. She wondered what Sacha really thought about it, for of course, someone like Claire would be proficient in all the sports— horseback riding, skiing, swimming——

'Well, you're damned sure going to learn how, now! *Right now!* My God, Katie, no wonder Kim was so frightened. He's picked up your panic! He can watch while you get your first lesson.'

'I can't, Sacha,' Katie said simply. 'I'm scared.'

'Daddy won't let you drown, Mommy,' Kim consoled her.

'I don't think I can do it,' Katie moaned.

'Get in here!' Sacha roared.

Katie jumped and did as he said, although she was panicky when Sacha gripped her hand and towed her out into slightly deeper water.

'Don't clutch me so,' he scolded, but gently, as though he really wasn't as angry as he had sounded. Finally, with an undertone of laughter, he added, 'Katie honey, if you don't stop clinging to me like that, we aren't going to get around to a lesson. I can't keep my mind on what I'm doing.'

'I can't help it, Sacha,' she panted, clinging to him like a little limpet. Her legs were wrapped around one of his thighs and her arms around his waist. She raised a stricken face from the wet, matted curls. 'I'm scared to death.'

'I know you are, darling,' he soothed. 'But try to relax.

Just stretch out and let the water hold you up. I'll keep my arms under you. You don't have to do a thing but float.'

Cautiously she followed his directions, struggling to conquer her panic so that she wouldn't frighten Kim. She found that Sacha projected an enormously reassuring sense of security. She stretched out gingerly and lowered the back of her head into the water, and finally, to her own amazement, she was floating.

'Good girl,' Sacha said approvingly. 'We'll have another lesson tomorrow. You and Kim.'

Suddenly Katie was supremely happy. She smiled delightedly and put her hands on Sacha's shoulders. Placing his hands under her arms, he lifted her out of the pool, his lips lightly brushing her breasts and leaving a trail of tingling fire. She drew a sharp breath, but Sacha had already turned away, his face an expressionless mask.

Suddenly a slim tanned body made a graceful arch through the air and entered the water within a couple of feet of Sacha. It was Claire, and as her body was buoyed upward, Katie saw that she was wearing a clinging 'wet look' binkini that barely covered the necessary spots.

Katie scrambled hurriedly to her feet. Kim's horse had been picked up this afternoon, and obviously Claire had expected Sacha to make the pick-up. When he hadn't been on the truck, she had got over here as fast as she could, perhaps bringing a bathing suit with her, in case. Or perhaps, Katie thought cynically, she keeps a bathing suit like that over here all the time.

'Hullo!' Claire raised a friendly hand at Katie. 'Am I interrupting something? Did my eyes decieve me, Sacha, or were you teaching your wife to swim?'

He grinned. 'The child never learned,' he agreed, apparently without the slightest idea of the humiliation Katie was feeling. 'I'm trying to teach both of them, and you're just in time to help with Kim. He needs someone to show him his strokes, and you're my gal.'

'Oh, I'd love to help! Hello, my little rabbit,' Claire breathed to a dazzled Kim. 'Will you come swim with me?'

As though he was hypnotised, Kim held out his arms obediently and slid off the poolside into Claire's waiting arms.

'The little devil!' Sacha laughed. 'He screamed blue murder when I tried to get him to come in!'

'He couldn't help it, Sacha. Katie's nervousness is bound to affect him,' said Claire, her eyes wide and sincere. 'Actually, it might be wise to teach Kim to swim first, then he can get a kick out of showing his mom how it's done.' Having buried her subtle seed, Claire then turned her attention to Kim. 'Oh, you're a darling! I love you!' She buried her beautiful face in his neck and Kim giggled.

Like the traitor he is, Katie thought sourly, and was immediately ashamed of herself. Kim couldn't help but succumb to Claire's blandishments and charm. He was a man, wasn't he?

She turned away droopingly, unnoticed by Sacha and Kim. She'd only make fool of herself if she stayed here. Competing with Claire in her own arena, astride a horse, in a pool, would be an exercise in futility. But there were other ways, Katie promised herself grimly as she left the pool. Claire, in spite of her boasted superiority, wasn't yet Sacha's wife. Katie held the trump card there, and she intended to take advantage of that fact before she gave him up to Claire for the mere asking.

CHAPTER SIX

STANDING before the mirror, putting on the last of her make-up, Katie felt nervously unsure of herself. The occasion, if one could call this dinner that, did not promise to be a pleasant one, which made it all the more important that she did justice to herself. She had debated over her sparse selection of clothes before deciding upon one of her own patchwork skirts. Unlike Claire's, Katie's skirt was rather muted, with brilliant hues of blues shading into vivid lavenders and pinks. With it she wore a blouse of pearl-pink silk. She had washed her hair after the swim and brushed it until it was as smooth and shiny as silk floss, then twisted it into a smooth coil on top of her head. The style suited her, showing off the classical shape of her profile and her small, delicate ears. She had decided to shoot the works on make-up and make an exception of her usual habit of wearing no more than a touch of lipstick and mascara. She had applied perfume three times, waiting each time until it had dried before re-daubing it at pulse points and in her hair. Then had come her eyes, a mauve eyeshadow blending into silver and a creamy bronze, then liner and mascara. Her foundation had blended her freckles into her tan, obliterating her milkmaid image. A touch of blusher added sparkle to her eyes, and her lips were outlined into a pouting fullness with a new wet-look lipstick, called 'Pouting Pink'. Leaning forward, she frowned slightly and increased the inviting curve of her mouth.

'I don't like it.'

Katie jumped, slashing her chin with pink.

'Do you have to creep up on me like that?' she demanded crossly. 'You scared me to death!' She picked up a tissue and began to scrub her chin.

'I thought you might want company.' Sacha's eyes met hers in the mirror. He was dressed for the semi-tropical night in a combination of black trousers and white jacket that accentuated his lean, dark, good looks.

He was starting to turn away, but Katie called him back hastily. 'Sacha! Yes, I—I do want company. Thank you.'

He smiled slightly at her capitulation. 'You look very beautiful,' he said generously. 'But I don't like that lipstick. It isn't you. However,' he reached in a breast pocket, 'my father gave me this tonight to give to you. They were my mother's.' Nestled on the lid of blue velvet was a heart-shaped diamond pendant on a silver chain. With it was a pair of matching diamond earrings. 'Now *this* does look like you.' Sacha took the pendant out of the box and fastened it around her neck.

'Th-thank you,' Katie stammered. With trembling fingers she removed her fake pearl buttons and inserted the diamonds in her ears. 'I've never had anything so beautiful before.' She raised shining eyes to his.

'Certainly not from me,' he agreed lazily. He seemed amused by her delight. 'Poor little Katie, you didn't gain much from being married to me, did you? Your home was a stuffy little apartment, and all the time I owned the entire city block! Did you know that, I wonder? My mother gave it to me when I went to San Francisco to study art,' he added ironically. 'And your only piece of jewellery has been that plain gold wedding band you're still wearing.'

Katie rested it briefly against her flushed cheek. 'I didn't marry you for a house or jewellery,' she said in a subdued voice.

'No. We both know why we got married,' he said in a

pleasant voice. 'It was a strong mutual—er—itch for each other, complicated by the fact that you were a virgin and I had a conscience.'

Katie was stung by his cool acknowledgement of what was no more than what she had admitted to Pat the day before.

'You didn't have to marry me. I didn't hold a gun to your head,' she flared defensively.

'No, not precisely. But I think you underestimate your effect on my senses, Katie. We've always had this strong physical thing between us. It's still there—to the point, in fact, that if we weren't due downstairs right now, I'd be tempted to tumble you upon that bed and prove it to you.'

For a moment his eyes lit with a look of naked desire. Katie trembled, unable to move. Her limbs were drugged with a lethargic sweetness—her body could feel his hands although he hadn't touched her. Catching her lower lip nervously between her teeth, she made a valiant effort to throw off the sensual effect of his words.

'Sacha, I—please, there's more to it than that. Than just—lust. There has to be love, too, for it to be good.'

'Indeed? And you don't think there's love, Katie?' He sounded idly curious.

'Well, only on one side.' Her little face tightened into a pinched mask. She had said enough, all that she intended to, for one night. She had no intention of further baring her soul for his amusement.

'I see. You *are* greedy, Katie. Personally, I think that would be enough to build on.'

'It would be hard on—the one who—loved.' Her voice shook, thinking just how hard it would be. How hard it *had* been.

'Well, it all sounds too complicated a subject when we're overdue for dinner.' He sounded bored. 'Claire and her father will be waiting, so let's get down before my grandmother sends for us.'

Katie felt snubbed. She followed him out of the room, her face flushed with humiliation. Obviously he wanted her and was prepared to build a marriage on just that and her love for him. But he had certainly made it clear that his feeling for her was sexual only. For the first time Katie faced up to it—that this might be all she would ever have. Why continue to hope for more? Why not accept the only thing he could give her, because oh, God, she thought desperately, I can't give him up! But am I justified in buying my own happiness at the expense of his and Claire's?

As they entered the room, Paul looked up from where he was dispensing drinks and gave her an encouraging smile. It was a little vote of confidence that Katie needed, for he was the only friend she was likely to have here tonight. She saw Madam Kimberly in her wheelchair, talking to Claire. This time, her muu-muu was of heavy white silk, rich with gold embroidery and lace. The loose sleeves fell away from the elbows to reveal diamond brace-lets on each arm. A number of gold chains, one of linked diamonds, circled the wrinkled old neck.

Claire showed no sign of the afternoon swim. Her black hair was shiny-smooth and she wore a delicate lacy spray of pearls and diamonds in it. Her dress was simple and seductive, ivory banded with gold at the V-shaped neck-line. The knife-pleated skirt was short and swingy and showed off her long, slim legs.

At the sight of Katie, her eyebrows arched slightly as though she questioned her choice of clothes. Her eyes lingered on the necklace and ear-rings, then she smiled slowly.

'How—sweet you look,' she drawled. 'And in one of your own skirts, too. What a charming idea!'

If Katie had been less selfconscious, she would have seen

that Claire's spitefulness stemmed from her shock at Katie's appearance, but Katie, already insecure, felt her self-confidence plunge.

Claire slipped a possessive arm under Sacha's elbow and cooed in his ear, 'Darling, did Kim like his horse?'

'He did,' Sacha grinned. 'I could hardly tear him away tonight.'

'Oh, he has all the instincts of a good horseman. I wonder—will it be all right if I run upstairs and see him? Will you take me?'

'Better not. He may be asleep, and besides, Katie hasn't met your father yet.'

Benjamin Thorpe was not the bloated, lecherous tycoon Katie had expected but a trim, handsome man with greying hair and a pair of dark, humorous eyes. Whatever his daughter might think of Katie, it was immediately clear that he was charmed with her. Katie was temporarily stunned to realise for the first time who he really was—the owner of one of the most famous art collections in the world. His name was a formidable one in Sacha's world—the world Katie had once aspired to.

'How do you do, Mr Thorpe?' she murmured uneasily.

'I can't allow a beautiful woman to call me that! You must call me Ben,' he commanded smilingly, taking her hand.

Obviously he was a man appreciative of femininity, but also a man used to getting his own way. He had passed on to his daughter that arrogance and self-confidence, along with a good share of his good looks. Plus all that money Katie added dismally. And money had a depressing habit of marrying money. Tonight Katie had learned just what Claire could offer the man she loved in addition to that—the support of her father, a recognised authority on modern art. No wonder she had confidently predicted that, given time, she would have Sacha.

Suddenly she realised that while Paul was taking orders for drinks, there had been a gradual re-shuffling, and somehow Claire had managed to draw Sacha away, leaving Katie standing alone with Benjamin Thorpe.

'I feel as though I know you already, Katie,' he commented. 'Because of *Dreaming*,' he explained, as she looked puzzled. 'I was on the Board that made the decision about the Llewellyn prize, although frankly, my mind was made up as soon as I saw the canvas. I've often wondered, my dear, if Sacha painted what he saw or what he wanted to see.'

Katie flushed. 'I *did* pose for it,' she admitted awkwardly.

'Do you realise how many men envy him when they look at that painting?' he persisted, lowering his voice to an intimate murmur.

Katie cleared her throat embarrassedly. 'I didn't realise—that is, I saw it for the first time yesterday.'

'I wanted to buy it from Sacha. I even asked him to name his own price, but he wouldn't sell.'

'Sacha has some other paintings that are better.' Katie's discomfort grew. If she read the signs right, Mr Thorpe was flirting with her, in full view of Sacha and his family, not to mention Claire. Miserably she wondered if Claire had asked her father to divert her attention so that she would have a clear field with Sacha. 'I can't imagine why you would want that particular painting.'

'So that I can make myself believe that the girl in it belongs to me,' he answered promptly. 'So that I can dream that it's I whom she's looking at, and we've just finished making love.'

Katie reddened. He had had a lot of experience with this sort of innuendo, and she had had none. 'I don't think you should talk like that,' she muttered.

'Is Ben saying something he shouldn't?' It was Paul,

handing her the sherry she had asked for. 'You must watch him. He's an accomplished wife stealer.' There was a slight edge to his voice.

Ben looked amused. 'I'm simply exercising the privileges accorded a member of the family, Paul.' He chuckled at Katie's blank look. 'I was, for a brief period, Sacha's step-father,' he exaplained. 'In other words, I was once married to his mother.'

Katie drew in a sharp breath of surprise.

'Only for a year or two,' Ben added, swirling the liquid in his glass reflectively. 'That's about the life of Marjorie's husbands. The lady is strong stuff.'

Katie wondered with a lurching heart if Sacha could ever talk about her that way, in that terribly indifferent, bored manner. If Ben was the cause of the break-up between Sacha's parents, that might explain Paul's slightly chilly attitude, although they had apparently remained friends.

'Then that makes Sacha and Claire a sort of brother and sister,' she said wonderingly.

Ben laughed and even Paul smiled slightly. 'I assure you, my dear, Claire doesn't feel sisterly,' Ben said wickedly.

Paul didn't like that. He frowned and made a protesting movement, as though he disapproved of his guest's blunt speaking. But at that moment dinner was announced, and Ben annexed Katie with a firmness that ignored all opposition. As Sacha came forward to wheel his grandmother into the dining room, he threw her a cold look that bewildered her. What she had done to merit such disapproval, she didn't know, unless he thought she was monopolising too much of Ben's attention. But Katie could have told him that one did not stop Ben Thorpe; he did just as he pleased. Already she knew that much about him.

The table was set with priceless antique Imari china,

with a low, Chinese red lacquer bowl containing white orchids in the centre. The seating arrangement was informal, allowing the conversation to be general. Katie soon saw that Claire had every intention of excluding her from the conversation, but she reckoned without her own father. His daughter might have her own axe to grind, but no one manipulated Benjamin Thorpe. He intended to talk to Katie even if it meant speaking across everyone's heads. Finally he pushed his glass aside and spoke directly to Sacha.

'Sacha, I want to commission you to do a painting. Name your own price. I make only one stipulation: Katie must be in it.'

Katie saw with a thrill of alarm that Sacha was furious. 'My wife is not a model.'

'She was your model for several of your earlier paintings,' Ben interposed sharply.

'None of which are out of my possession, if you notice,' Sacha replied grittily. 'I paint my wife for my own pleasure, not for anyone else's.'

'What a singularly unaccommodating chap you are, to be sure,' Ben said softly. 'It's unwise for a young artist to be so stiffnecked.' It was a veiled threat.

'You have my permission to reject anything of mine you wish to.'

Ben laughed spontaneously. 'Reject? Hardly that. No, on the contrary, I buy up everything of yours I can lay my hands on.'

There was a general laugh and the tense moment passed, but Ben referred to it again as they were making their farewells.

'Since you won't allow me to have a painting of Katie, perhaps you'll allow her to accompany me to the Club one afternoon for a drink?'

Sacha was poker-faced. 'That's up to Katie.'

Katie felt a flash of pique. Did he have to make his indifference so obvious? Smiling sweetly at Ben, she drawled, 'I'd love to go.'

When the door closed behind the departing guests Katie excused herself and fled upstairs. She had managed to pass the whole evening without addressing a single direct word to Madam Kimberly or Claire, and the effort had exhausted her.

She went wearily into her bedroom, where she stripped herself of her clothes. Skirt, blouse, stockings and high-heeled sandals followed one another in a pile on the floor. Then, in bra and bikini panties, she went into the bathroom. What I need is a long soak in a warm tub and maybe, while I'm soaking, she thought wryly, I can get my head together. Leaning over the tub, she turned on the water, then adjusted the taps to the right temperature. A cloud of steam arose and she shook bubble powder into the flow, and watched it foam up into pearly suds. It mounted higher and higher until it came up almost to the level of the edge of the tub, and Katie hastily turned off the taps. Something about the waiting stillness alerted her, and she turned quickly to find Sacha leaning casually against the bathroom door, watching her.

'What are you doing here?' she asked sharply. She was very conscious of her near-nakedness and she shrank back against the edge of the tub.

'Looking for you.'

Katie swallowed convulsively. 'Well, now that you've found me, perhaps you'll let me slip on a robe.' She looked around warily for something to cover her nakedness.

'Nope.' He settled himself comfortably against the door. 'I like you better the way you are.' He was probably naked, too, under his dark blue robe, which was belted loosely about his wast, giving a disturbing glimpse of a bare chest and legs.

'Wh-what did you want to talk to me about?' she asked faintly.

Before he could reply, there was a rap at her bedroom door. 'Mr Sacha, you in there?'

He turned away, muttering an oath half under his breath, and strode towards the door. Katie, straining her ears to listen, heard him open the door violently and ask curtly, 'What do you want, Oola?'

'It Miss Claire, sir. She come back just now, have some horse papers she say you must have. Madam say for me to fetch you.'

It was the first time Katie had heard Oola's voice, which was a high-pitched sing-song.

Sacha swore. 'For God's sake, Oola! Those papers can wait. Tell my grandmother that I'm already undressed and ready for bed. I'll see Claire in the morning.'

'Yes, sir.'

Katie had lost her opportunity to escape from the bathroom. She was fiddling nervously with the bath taps when Sacha returned. She had been highly gratified by the brusque message he had sent to Claire, by way of his grandmother, and she was wearing a flush of excitement that brightened her eyes. He eyed her amusedly.

'At one time you would have been waiting for me in the bathtub,' he murmured silkily.

The blush deepened. 'Sacha!' she protested breathlessly. 'Sometimes I—I—feel as though you are a stranger.'

'A stranger?' He raised an eyebrow questioningly.

'Well—not my husband. It's been so long, you can't—I mean, how can you expect me to act as though nothing had happened? As though we'd been living together all along,' she explained confusedly.

'Are you trying to raise a barricade of objections again?' he asked, moving towards her purposefully.

Katie left the vicinity of the tub hurriedly, sure that he had every intention of dunking her in, and began to sidle along the wall towards the door. Halfway there, Sacha captured her by the simple expedient of putting both palms on the wall and pinning her firmly between them.

'My mistake has been in giving you too much time,' he growled huskily. 'I thought you needed it, and I didn't want to rush you, but——' He broke off to nuzzle her hair. He was very close, close enough for their breaths to mingle, but he did not touch her. Her hands were wet, and she flattened them desperately against the wall, the nails digging into the cool tiles as though seeking an escape behind her.

'I do.' She shivered, although she was burning with heat. 'I do need time——'

'No,' he contradicted her softly. His breath fanned the hair at her temples. 'I know you, Katie. It's fatal to give you time to regroup your defences. I should have followed my first instinct and taken you at once. When our reconcilation has become an established fact, you'll feel less tetchy about it.'

'About—it?'

'About our making love.' Sacha's mouth quirked and Katie watched it fascinatedly. 'You're torn, Katie, between wanting me and what you probably think of as your better nature. In other words, that prim, inhibited side of you.'

His lips touched her ear, then he lightly bit the delicate lobe before running his tongue along the outer curl. It was an unbelievably erotic sensation, and Katie thought dizzily that her better nature had just given up with a whimper of defeat. She closed her eyes as his exploring mouth trailed down her throat and found the pulse that beat frantically at its base. A warm tongue tested its vibrating heat, and she turned her head restlessly, her lips blindly seeking his.

'Sacha,' she murmured urgently.

'Want me?' he teased, then kissed her. It was a caress so feathery soft that Katie could have broken the contact by merely moving her head slightly. In fact, he was not touching her, but letting his lips speak for him in the age-old language of the kiss.

Every scared thought, every objection, fled Katie's mind as she responded to the unbearable sweetness of his lips. She parted her lips tremblingly, and the kiss deepened. Unconsciously, she swayed closer, and Sacha gathered her into his arms, allowing her to feel the thrusting hardness of his body. She was racked by such a wave of intense longing that instinctively her body arched, moulding its soft contours to his hard-muscled frame.

'Say you want me,' he whispered against her lips.

Katie moaned softly, 'Sacha, please——'

'Say it.'

'I want you——' she repeated raggedly.

'Sacha, I want you to make love to me.'

'Sacha—Sacha——' Restlessly, Katie groped and burrowed beneath the open throat of his robe, her lips seeking the hair-roughened chest.

'Put your arms around me.'

With the mindless obedience of a robot, Katie's arms encircled his neck. He bent and lifted her swiftly, then carried her into the bedroom. As he was lowering her to the bed, Katie grew aware of a distant pounding and calling.

'Mr Sacha! Mr Sacha!'

Sacha swore softly under his breath and loosened his arms reluctantly.

'What's wrong, Yoshura?' he called.

The Japanese houseman must have moved to Katie's door, for his voice was stronger, louder.

'It's the old madam, sir. She say you to come. Quick!'

'Why?' Is she ill?'

'I not know, Mr Sacha. Miss Claire say she sick. She say you to come quick.'

Sacha swore again. 'I'll be there as soon as I get on something.' He turned back to Katie. 'I'm sorry, darling. I'll be right back as soon as I see what the trouble is.'

Katie felt as though she had been slapped. She was totally vulnerable now, still trembling in the aftermath of her overwhelming need.

'There's no trouble!' she burst out irrationally. 'They know you're here with me, and they want to get you away!'

'Don't be silly.' Sacha's hands were gentle as he disengaged her clinging fingers. 'Something is wrong. Grandmother may be ill.'

Katie wanted to scream. She was appalled at the ease with which he had crumpled her defences. She could not even accuse him of forcing her, for she had begged him to take her, but now he could leave her just as easily, at the first snap of his grandmother's fingers. Horrified, she heard herself begging, 'Sacha, don't go! Stay with me! Show me that you want me more than you want her—them!'

He glanced at her impatiently. 'You're being childish!' he said crisply. 'Of course I want you—but my grand-mother——'

'I know about your grandmother!' she broke in passionately. 'She wants you to marry Claire, and she'll do anything to part us! She's pretending to be ill, so that she can get you out of this bedroom! Oola—Oola went downstairs and—told her where you were, and——'

'Shut up!' A thin line of white around his mouth showed the violence of his anger. 'You're jealous and resentful and petty! I thought you'd changed, that you'd grown up, but you haven't. You're still full of delusions and fantasies that are fed by your own spiteful, mean little nature! My grandmother is incapable of the sort of behaviour you're talking about. Now, get yourself together, Katie. I'm going downstairs, and if I find that it's nothing, I'll be back. Otherwise, I won't!'

Katie huddled back against the headboard of the bed. She hurt—all over—as though Sacha's hard words had been sticks that had beaten her. There was only one thing to be said, and she said it.

'If you do come back, don't bother to try the door. It will be locked.'

An ugly look crossed his face. 'I don't intend to go through this again,' he warned her icily. 'A warmed-over reconciliation is about as indigestible as warmed-over food. Next time you're going to have to beg for me a lot harder than you did five years ago.'

Katie flinched, sickened by the reminder of her abject pleading. He had turned his back on her then, too. Her humiliation was complete.

'Please go,' she said shakily.

With an angry expletive he left her, slamming the door behind him. Shivering, Katie buried her face into the pillow. From heaven to hell in one swift leap, she thought dully. Where did she come in Sacha's affections, anyway? How far down the ladder?

She forgot her threat to lock the door, but finally, after a long time had passed, she burrowed beneath the sheet. If Madam was really ill, someone would go for the doctor, and since her bedroom overlooked the garages, she should hear the car when it drove out. But there was no sound from there. Unless Claire went in her car? Katie huddled, listening vainly for noises that would indicate what was happening. She still did not doubt her instincts that there had been nothing wrong with Madam, but as time went on, and Sacha's footsteps did not go past her door, she began to wonder if she could have been mistaken. And if she was, she knew desolately that Sacha would never forgive her.

Suddenly Katie was brought upright by the sound of a slamming door, a car motor, voices, all below her window. She ran over in time to see Sacha handing Claire into the back seat of one of the ranch cars. It was being driven by one of the ranch hands. Claire was still dressed as she had been earlier and Sacha had apparently slipped on a shirt and slacks before going downstairs. Claire was laughing about something, and Sacha's answering laugh floated up to Katie through the open window.

He stood at the window of the car and talked for another minute before waving them away. After a suitable interval Katie heard his footsteps along the corridor, then the sound of his closing door. He had not bothered to try her door. She lay in bed, dry-eyed, until dawn, then fell into a restless sleep.

CHAPTER SEVEN

FOR the second morning in a row, Katie overslept. She dressed hurriedly in a loose silk blouse with matching skirt before looking into Kim's room. It was empty; the drawers had been pulled out and the clothes tumbled as though a small whirlwind had wrecked itself on the room. Apparently he had been awakened and taken downstairs by Sacha. Katie stood hesitantly before Sacha's door before finally knocking and then, looking in. It was empty, too.

Downstairs, she looked uncertainly around the cold, silent dining room.

'Missy want breakfast?' Yoshura materialised at her elbow.

'Y-yes, please. Where is everyone?'

'Mr Paul out in fields; Mr Sacha with Kim at stables. Family eat breakfast in this room,' he added, leading her into a smaller dining room, informally furnished with wicker and yellow pottery. Chairs were still pushed back, as though the room had just been vacated.

'This is—nice. Everything seems so quiet this morning,' she added tentatively.

'Old Madam had attack last night,' Yoshura replied, piling dirty dishes on a tray. 'You want bacon—eggs, maybe?'

'An attack? You mean—a heart attack?'

'No. Stomach, I think. You not know?'

She shook her head numbly.

'When Missy Claire leave last night, she come back with some papers. While she here, Old Madam get sick. She send for Oola to tell me to fetch Mr Sacha.'

Katie's cheeks had paled. 'Oh, God,' she thought sickly, 'he was right, and I *have* been a criminally jealous fool!' Aloud she asked, 'What did the doctor say about it?'

Yoshura shook his head. 'No doctor. She no want doctor. Just Missy Claire and Mr Sacha.'

Something odd in his voice made Katie ask, 'Did you see her, Yoshura?'

He gave a gigantic shrug. 'I no see her. Just Oola. No want Mr Paul, just Mr Sacha,' he added expressionlessly. Abruptly, he left the room, carrying the loaded tray.

After breakfast Katie knocked timidly at Madam Kimberly's door, prepared to eat crow if Sacha was in there with his grandmother. The door was opened a cautious slit by Oola.

'I just learned that Madam was taken ill last night,' Katie explained anxiously. 'May I see her, please?'

'No see her,' Oola replied flatly.

'But surely——'

'No see her,' Oola repeated. 'Missy Claire with her now.'

'Is she worse, then?' Katie asked. 'Has the doctor been to see her? What did he say?'

'Who is it, Oola?' It was Claire's voice, brisk and assured.

Oola looked over her shoulder. 'Missy Katie. She want to know why you no send for doctor.'

The door, released by Oola, swung open slowly, and Katie could see into the sickroom. The bed was empty, but a card table had been pulled up to it, and Madam Kimberly and Claire were seated at it, with a hand of gin rummy spread out before them. Madam was also drinking a cup of coffee and her head was wreathed in smoke from the cigarette she was holding. She did not look ill, and from the expression of consternation that spread over her face when she looked up and saw Katie, it was obvious that she was aware of the impression she was giving.

'Get her out of here!' she commanded, with a moan of distress. 'Claire, please——! I'm too weak to cope with anyone just now——'

'I'll see to it,' Claire murmured soothingly.

Outside, in the hallway, with the door closed firmly behind her, Claire faced Katie determinedly.

'What's this all about?' she asked crisply. 'Madam Kimberly is very ill—she mustn't be disturbed. Can't you leave her alone?'

Katie opened her mouth to indignantly protest her innocence, then closed it again. 'How ill is she?' she asked shrewdly. 'Has she seen a doctor?'

Claire flushed. 'How dare you?' she hissed. 'How dare you suggest that she's not ill? That last night was a put-up job between us!'

Katie blinked. She had only meant to suggest that Madam's illness had been exaggerated, but as soon as Claire spoke, she realised that her defensiveness was motivated by fear—fear that Katie had guessed the truth and might be able to persuade Sacha of it.

'Was it a put-up job?' she asked gently.

'Of course not!' Claire wouldn't meet her eyes. 'You have a nasty, suspicious mind to think such a thing! Just wait until I tell Sacha's grandmother what you've accused her of——'

'I thought she was too ill to be disturbed,' Katie said mildly.

Claire's eyes flashed. 'Go away!' she snapped, and flounced back into the bedroom.

Katie stared blankly at the slammed door, trying to recover herself by drawing steadying breaths.

'What's the matter? Is my mother worse?' It was Paul, and in spite of his anxious question he was smiling quizzically at her. 'What are you doing outside her door, looking as though you've been thrown out! Is that what happened, Katie?'

'No—no——' she stammered. 'I think she may be better this morning.'

He nodded calmly. 'Probably. These attacks don't last long.'

'Then she's had them before?'

'Frequently. And will continue to, so long as she's a glutton and eats the kind of heavy meals she ate last night. The doctor has warned her—— In fact, this might be a good time, while she's—er—temporarily indisposed, for you to take charge of the house, Katie. Particularly the menus.' He grinned conspiratorially. 'My mother needs to be put on a sensible diet, because she's too fond of rich, spicy foods. Perhaps you could do something along the line of what you mentioned yesterday and plan the menus to include a better diet for my mother. What about it?'

Katie hesitated. 'Of course I would—but I don't think your mother will like it. The cook won't——'

'Mrs O'Connor will do whatever you say so long as she knows you're acting under my orders,' he replied crisply.

'But your mother won't like it,' she reminded him. 'I think you should know—she wouldn't mind Claire interfering, but not me——'

'This is my house, Katie, and my mother merely resides here. If I ask you to supervise the kitchen, then it's my privilege to do so. I'll back up anything you want to do.' Paul added, picking his words carefully, 'Claire Wetherell isn't Sacha's wife: you are. It's my dearest wish—and my mother's—for Sacha to live in Hawaii, but I can't see that happening if we make his wife feel a stranger in his home.'

Under the circumstances, Katie could hardly refuse. She made her way to the kitchen to confront the cook, whose skill could not be faulted. Every meal, so far, had been a culinary masterpiece. Last night's dinner would have done justice to an exclusive restaurant, and from the way Claire and her father had spoken, the Kimberly family was lucky to have her. The last thing Katie wanted to do was upset the cook and have her leave.

The room was empty except for a large, fat Hawaiian lady who was enjoying a mid-morning snack of coffee and pastry. When she saw Katie she surged to her feet, beaming.

'Sit down, Missy Katie. Sit down. I am glad you come to visit my kitchen. Have some coffee and a bun. How is Old Madam?'

Katie was taken aback. This was Mrs O'Connor? She was pressed into a chair and handed a cup of delicious coffee and a generous slice of coffee cake that was so rich and mouthwateringly good that it melted in her mouth.

'You won't keep Old Madam in bed, not that one.' The grin broadened. 'She never give up. She have arthritis so bad she almost no can walk, but she still boss.'

Katie proceeded delicately. 'Mr Paul hopes I will take some of the responsibilities off her shoulders for the time being,' she began. 'He asked me to help, and one of the ways is to—er—plan the menus with you. While she's ill, Madam Kimberly must have a bland diet.'

'That's right, that's right.' Mrs O'Connor nodded delightedly, as though she was encouraging a backward child. 'The doctor say I cook too spicy.'

Katie's jaw dropped. 'Then—you know——?'

'Missy Katie,' was the kindly assurance, '*I* cook whatever you say. *You* be the one to make Old Madam eat it. Okay?'

Katie gulped slightly. 'Then it will be difficult?'

Mrs O'Connor's eyes twinkled. 'We-e-ell, you'll have Mr Paul and Mr Sacha to help you.'

'Very well, Mrs O'Connor. You cook it and I'll see that she eats it!' Katie's eyes sparkled determinedly.

The cook broke into deep, satisfying laughter. 'Just you

keep Old Madam from blaming me!'

It took Katie a while to work out the week's menus with Mrs O'Connor's help. The meals were not to change that much, except for the rich, spicy casseroles and desserts. She found that Mrs O'Connor had a lot of ideas on how to vary them for a sick person's bland diet, which was not so surprising after Katie made the discovery that she had once been a hospital dietician. They were in perfect accord when Katie finally left her. As she emerged from the kitchen, she met Sacha on his way upstairs. He had just come from his grandmother's room and was looking for her; and she saw he was furious.

'I want to talk to you—in private.' He gripped her wrist and savagely yanked her into the study. 'I understand you called on my grandmother this morning?' he went on angrily, as soon as he had closed the door behind them.

'I called on her, yes. I was told that she was ill and it seemed only polite to ask about her. What's wrong with that?' she flashed.

'Nothing—if politeness was your reason,' he said grimly. 'To call on an elderly lady and enquire about her illness is kind, but then to subject her to an inquisition and insinuate that she's been lying merely because she's refused to see the doctor is vicious cruelty! I told you before, Katie,' he added coldly, ignoring her gasp of disbelief, 'I won't have you worrying my grandmother. Call me whatever names you like and accuse me of whatever infidelities you care to, but when it comes to Gran, keep your sick little fantasies to yourself! I won't have you disturbing her. In other words, I don't want you to go into her room again unless I'm with you. Is that clear?'

'Very clear.' Katie, white-faced, jerked her arm out of his iron grip. 'May I ask who told you all this?'

'Oh, come off it, Katie. You know it was Claire. She didn't want to do it, but she had to tell me. She knew you couldn't be allowed to upset my grandmother again like that.'

'Couldn't you have asked your grandmother if I upset her?'

His mouth compressed. 'I did. She said you'd insisted on a doctor because you didn't really believe she was ill. She may be a bit of a hypochondriac, but she's never had anyone call her a liar before! As a matter of fact, Claire and I had already decided that she should see a doctor, too, but we knew better than to put our suggestion like that. Gran is scared to death the doctor will put her into hospital, so she's hysterically opposed to having him called in. So I always call him quietly without telling her anything about it.'

'I see.' And Katie did. *Of course*, it sounded plausible —and why not? If she hadn't seen Madam Kimberly in such obvious good health, and if she hadn't caught that look of guilt before Madam began her swooning act, she would think her ill, too. As it was, she had been nipped in the bud, so to speak, by Claire reaching Sacha first with a story that made Katie seem suspicious and mean-minded. And Madam Kimberly had backed her to the hilt, so that Sacha believed whatever outrageous, vicious lie Claire chose to tell about her. Well, she knew where she stood now. She couldn't expect to have Sacha's loyalty when it conflicted with Claire's.

'Is that all?' she asked proudly.

He scowled. 'It is! I think you've done enough damage for one day. I hope you'll try to confine your activities to taking some of the burden of housekeeping off Gran's shoulders, particularly while she's ill. It seems the least you can do.'

'Very well.' She turned away.

'Under the circumstances,' he added, 'I should think

you'd have the decency to apologise for your suggestions last night.'

Katie turned back. He was regarding her frowningly with a vague look of dissatisfaction.

She was shaken by a storm of resentment that she could not control. 'Oh, no, Sacha!' she said bitterly, 'you can't have everything! I've agreed to stay away from your grandmother. I'll even stay away from Claire if you like, and I will certainly do the housekeeping. But you can't expect me to mouth words that I know are lies merely to satisfy your pride.'

His lip curled. 'I should have known you'd be too child-ish to acknowledge your mistakes. You still haven't grown up, have you, Katie?'

The next few days were hell for Katie. On the brighter side, there was the improvement in Kim. Overnight, it seemed, he had turned into a sturdy, self-reliant little boy, who was out all day—at the stables; in the pool; riding his tricycle; running through the house, shouting, with Sammy yapping at his heels. His activities were too numerous and varied to name. Katie was no longer the centre of his life; Sacha had assumed equal importance, and Katie had to admit that the change in Kim was due to the relationship with his father. The babyishness and clinging had dis-appeared now that he had a male figure to pattern himself on.

The child made a great difference to his grandfather, too, which was another bright score in Katie's ledger of accounts. Paul adored Kim, and gave credit to Katie in full for the child's sturdy independence and instinctive good manners. He also went out of his way to show that he liked and approved of her, too.

He had business associates who dropped in, frequently; they often stayed for lunch or dinner and sometimes were accompanied by their wives. As she was his hostess, Paul deferred to Katie and demonstrated clearly that he was pleased with his new daughter-in-law—which made a distinct change from Sacha's chill tolerance.

As the days passed and obviously Sacha still disapproved of her, it became difficult even to be in the same room with him. Katie became rather adept at avoiding occasions when she might be alone with him, and since the ranch was a big place, it was not too hard to do. She knew that he was seeing a lot of Claire, who was at the ranch every day, using as her excuse Kim's riding and swimming lessons.

As soon as Katie saw that Claire had every intention of being present for the swimming lessons, she dropped out. Rather than watch Claire's triumphant success with Kim and expose her own shortcomings, she elected to bow out, and from the way Sacha's lip curled when he asked her about it, she knew that he saw it merely as another instance of her cowardice and sick obsession with her fantasies.

That made it much more important to stick during the riding lessons. She reasoned that she could watch and encourage Kim without laying herself open to any of Claire's taunts. She arrived that first morning to find a highly efficient Claire alone with Kim and giving competent, crisp orders. Quite naturally, before too many days had passed Kim was turning to Claire rather than his mother when he did something well. It was Claire's praise that brought a big grin to his face, and one day, when he said impatiently, 'Oh, Mommy, you don't know anything about it!' Katie knew that he was merely echoing what he had overheard.

Her face must have reflected what she was feeling, for Sacha, who happened to be present for the first time that day, strolled over and said impatiently, 'Claire is an experienced teacher; she knows everything about this subject, and it's her opinion that Kim shouldn't be distracted by outsiders while he's having his lesson, so let's leave her to it, shall we?'

So Claire had managed to pry her out of her perilous clutch on the riding lessons, too. After that, Katie did not return.

During the week following her so-called attack. Katie did not see anything of Madam Kimberly. She had a good idea of the old lady's frame of mind. It must be extremely frustrating to know that Katie was now in charge of her home, and when news items filtered through by way of Oola of Katie's domestic activities, she made an attempt to assert herself by changing some of her orders. But Paul and the doctor stood firm. They may have had a pretty shrewd idea that Madam's illness was partially feigned, but she had played into their hands and now they were using the opportunity to force her to slow down.

One afternoon, Katie was particularly depressed—things had built up until she knew she had to get away; be alone and try to gain a reasonable perspective. She strolled off on her own, intending to follow the line of the electrified fence to the very end of the Kimberly property. As she walked she was struck, as usual, by the way the volcanic origins of the islands had provided Hawaii with some of the most panoramic scenery on earth. When she finally stopped, she was standing on a hill overlooking a valley of indescribable beauty. In the distance she could see a sweep of white sand, ringed by palm trees, ending in the sea. Glittering beneath the sun, it faded into a softer blue at the horizon's edge. In the nearer distance, the flat roofs of a large house nestled among the hills, and although she would need binoculars to be certain, she did not think it was the Kimberly house. Whose, then?

With a tired gesture Katie dropped to the ground and drew her knees up to rest beneath her chin. The clink of harness brought her head up swiftly and she saw a lone horseman approaching. It was Benjamin Thorpe.

'Hullo.' He smiled as he brought the horse to a halt and slid lithely to the ground. Looping the reins around a nearby bush, he strolled over to where she sat and dropped beside her. 'This *is* my lucky day! What brings you all this way?'

'I've been for a walk. Why? Am I very far from home?'

He whistled slightly beneath his breath. 'About three miles. You're on Thorpe land now.'

She frowned. 'I didn't cross the electronic fence.'

'That fence merely guards the house compound. There are miles of acreage that are unfenced. Not really very secure to anyone who approaches from our direction. Didn't you know?'

'No, I suppose not. You said this was Thorpe land,' she added hesitantly. 'You mean Wetherell land, surely?'

He laughed. 'Legally, it's Thorpe land. Mine. I support Claire. Wetherell didn't give her a cent. One can't blame him, poor devil, since the divorce was her idea.' He paused and eyed her with a cynical gleam. 'Aren't you going to ask me why?' he added wickedly.

'No,' Katie replied calmly, thinking how much like a small, naughty boy he sounded. 'But I have no doubt you're going to tell me.'

He laughed. 'Touché! Obviously you know why. It doesn't worry you?'

'Of course not.' With an effort, Katie kept her voice light and uncaring, knowing that what she said would probably find its way back to Claire. 'What Claire wants has nothing to do with my life.'

'Most wives wouldn't be so—er—co-operative about sharing their husbands.'

'What do you mean?' she asked sharply.

'Sacha is at our house many nights. Surely you knew?' he asked blandly.

'No.' Katie thought of the nights when Sacha disappeared immediately after dinner. She had thought he was in his studio, because lately he had begun to paint again.

'Sacha has always been close to Claire. I think you said once—like brother and sister.' The voice held a thread of amusement. 'Of course, I don't know what happens when I go to bed and leave them. Perhaps—just more talk——' he paused mischievously.

Katie turned away abruptly, hiding her face from him, her nails biting deep into her palms as she tried to stiffen herself against the pictures that began to unfold in her mind. Truly, Benjamin Thorpe was a master at the art of insinuation.

'You could do something about it, you know,' he said suggestively.

'What?' She turned back, her face naked to his sharpened eyes.

'Provide some competition. Let Sacha know that what's sauce for the gander is sauce for the goose, etc. It has been known to work.'

'I don't believe in playing games with people's feelings.'

'Not even to save your marriage?'

'No, thank you.'

'Well, if you should change your mind, I'll be glad to co-operate.' His voice roughened. 'Oh, yes, indeed, I'll be glad to co-operate.'

'Is that your horse or Claire's?' Katie asked, in an effort to lighten the atmosphere, which had suddenly grown taut with tension.

'It's mine when I visit Claire, although one of the hands exercises it when I'm not here. The brute's much too strong for Claire to ride. Will you ask Sacha to sell me *Dreaming*?' Ben added abruptly.

She burst into laughter. 'You *are* persistent, aren't you?'

'My dear, of course. I never give up when it's someone I want as badly as I want you.'

She sobered instantly. 'I thought we were talking about a painting?'

'You don't really think we are, do you?' His eyes held a twinkle as they roved over her uneasy face. 'I'm lost in admiration of the painting, but I would be stupid to prefer it over the real thing. Quite suddenly, it's occurred to me that I might have such an opportunity. You're not a fool— you must know that I want you.' His voice roughened. 'Would you be interested in accepting me as your lover? I wouldn't insult you by citing the material advantages to you—although there are many, but I know that wouldn't weigh. But I promise you would find me a considerate, skilful lover.'

'No, Ben. If it ever comes to that point, it will only be because I don't have a marriage or a husband.'

'Naturally,' he said dryly, without belabouring the obvious point. 'It was merely a thought, and I hope you won't allow it to distress you until you're ready to think of it again.'

He rose then and prepared to take his leave. Together they walked over to the horse. There was no trace of embarrassment in his manner as he talked lightly before springing up into the saddle, and Katie began to wonder if she had dreamed that this man had just asked her to become his mistress, and although there had been no word about love, he had certainly made it clear that he desired her. However, when he leaned down from the saddle to take her hand before departing, she caught a naked look in his eyes that made her shiver slightly, and she was reminded forcibly of Benjamin Thorpe's reputation for getting what he went after.

The next morning Claire deliberately sought her out

while she was in the breakfast room polishing silver. Claire was wearing jodhpurs and, from the trace of dampness on her forehead, had apparently just come from Kim's riding lesson.

'I want to talk to you,' she said abruptly.

Katie rose and followed Claire, who led the way into the study with as much assurance as though she was the lady of the house. Standing with her back to the desk, she faced Katie, her exotic beauty a flaming contrast to the sombreness of the room.

'I want you to stay away from my father,' she drawled insolently. Katie opened her mouth, but Claire forestalled her. 'Oh, don't try to deny it. I know you met him yesterday—and on *my* land! You'd done your homework well, and found out that he was in the habit to taking that ride every day!'

'I have no intention of denying it,' Katie replied. Her cheeks were flying red flags of anger, but she kept her voice steady with an effort. 'Why should I? The meeting was accidental. If he told you about it, he surely made that clear to you.'

'As a matter of fact, he didn't tell me about it. One of my ranch hands saw you and mentioned it to me. My father is not given to talking about the details of his—er—affairs to me,' Claire added insultingly.

Katie clenched her fist to avoid slapping the beautiful, haughty face. 'Then I suggest you ask him about it, unless you're afraid he might tell you to mind your own business!'

'Which is exactly what he would do!' Claire laughed brittlely. 'He doesn't like my interference when he's pursuing a woman, but I know him too well. I saw that he was attracted to you the moment he met you, and of course, he would understand that you would be at a loose end when Sacha gets a divorce.'

'You seem certain that he will.'

Claire's eyes glittered. 'I assure you that he will. He's on the point now of asking you to live apart from him, and when he does—— Where are you going?' Her voice changed sharply.

'Out of here. Away from you. I don't intend to listen to this.'

'Oh, no, you're not!' With a leap, Claire was at the door, barring the way, her blazing eyes and flushed face showing her emotion. Katie eyed her measuringly. They were the same height and she wondered if Claire could prevent her from leaving if she made an attempt to do so. Claire's eyes narrowed slightly as she read her thoughts. 'Don't try it,' she said dangerously. 'I'm stronger than you, and I don't intend to let you leave until you hear me out.'

'Say it, then,' Katie said boredly.

Claire looked slightly disconcerted. 'I won't allow you to get your hot little hands on my father and his money!'

'Which is what you're really concerned about, isn't it?' Katie mused. 'I wonder how he'd like it if he knew you'd taken a hand in his so-called pursuit of me?' Claire's face whitened and Katie knew she had struck a nerve. She pressed on. 'You said he doesn't like interference, and I suspect he can be quite ruthless if you displease him. As ruthless as you are yourself, perhaps. He told me that he supported you, which must mean that you're dependent upon his good will. And I don't think we're talking about your father making me his mistress, are we, Claire? You must be used to that situation by now. But you're afraid that he might want to marry again, particularly if it's to a young woman who might have a child. For some reason, you suspect that he might enjoy the opportunity to cut you out of your inheritance, don't you, Claire?' she added, making an inspired guess. She saw by Claire's face that her reasoning was correct. 'What's the matter, Claire? Isn't Sacha's money enough for you—or can it be that you aren't so sure of Sacha as you say you are?'

Claire fumbled with the door knob, then flung the door open. Her face was twisted with rage and fear. 'Get out!' she hissed, in a low, throaty voice. 'Get out of here before I slap that smirk off your face. I—hate you!'

For once in their many one-sided encounters, Katie had got the best of her enemy. Head high, she strolled out, her bearing insolent and triumphant. She felt good; in fact, she felt wonderful.

'Don't worry, Katie, I'm coping, although I'm overwhelmed with admiration at the way you managed this shop and a child singlehanded except for an occasional assist from me. How did you do it?' Pat's voice, over the telephone, was as welcome as a drink of water in the midst of a parched desert.

'All by sleight of hand, my dear.' By trying very hard, Katie was able to make her voice sound light. 'Then you don't need me at all?' She hated to push, but she desperately needed a bolthole—some place to go where she could gain a breathing space away from the oppressive atmosphere of this house. Not that Sacha would believe that it was necessary to dart over to Oahu at the drop of a crisis, but just the same, if there had been an honest to goodness one. . . . Although nothing had been said about putting a car at her service, and considering that a trip to Honolulu would mean complicated travelling arrangements, it was perhaps expecting too much of Sacha that he would agree to her leaving to help Pat out at the shop.

'You must be having a wonderful time,' Pat went on blithely, oblivious to the irony of her words for Katie. 'Everyone has been telling me how lucky you are.'

'E-everyone?'

'All the people who've been crowding into the shop the last few days!' Pat's laughter was rich with delight. 'Honestly, Katie! You'd be amazed at the customers I've had—and all of them dying to learn something about you! I had no idea that your husband's people were so important. Did you?'

'N-no.'

'Well, they are. Hawaiian aristocrats, if there's such a thing. They've been here since the year One and your papa-in-law owns a good slice of Hawaiian real estate, plus having his finger in quite a few pies, businesswise. What's the house like?'

'Fabulous,' Katie said weakly.

'That's what everyone says,' Pat agreed. 'I've been hearing quite a bit about the Kimberlys this week. Everyone seems to know about you—that you're over there in the family home, living with your husband again but they've all made excuses to drop by the shop, and while they're here, quizzing me about you, they're shopping. Katie,' Pat's voice dropped dramatically, 'what's this about Claire Wetherell?'

'What about her?'

'Several of the women have been more than willing to talk about her. Seems that she's a beauty, who's had her eye on Sacha for years. Her father married Sacha's mother—in fact, the story goes that he broke up her marriage to Sacha's father. Well, when the split-up came and the remarriage, Claire was a little girl, and Sacha sort of took her under his wing. Her mother was dead, and her father too busy to care about her, and of course, *his* mother's solution to the whole problem was to put her in a boarding school and forget all about her. Well, big brother Sacha sort of adopted her. During summer vacations, when he came to Hawaii to see his people, she came along. No one cared about her at home.

Anyway, she was like one of the family, and when she got her divorce from Tony Wetherell, she bought the place next door to the Kimberlys. She'd always loved horses and that's what she's doing, breeding horses and keeping in touch with Sacha through his father and grand-mother.'

'I see.' Somehow, hearing the whole story like this, it seemed much more plausible—and more depressing. Sacha's attitude towards Claire, for instance, *was* one of protectiveness, and apparently it stemmed from events of their childhood. How could he, therefore, believe that she would lie to him, especially when compared to Katie, who he already believed was capable of any sort of childish, irrational behaviour to get her own way?

'They say it nearly killed her when Sacha married you. It wouldn't have happened if she hadn't been on a cruise or something at the time. Anyway, she immediately married Tony Wetherell, who'd been in love with her for ages, and divorced him just as quickly when she learned that Sacha's marriage had gone on the rocks. Er—Katie, is she hanging around?'

Katie was conscious of a hysterical desire to laugh. 'I—I think I can safely say that she is,' she replied carefully. And that is the understatement of the year, she added to herself.

'Well, honey, I hate to make you nervous on your second honeymoon, but forewarned is forearmed. Keep your eye on Claire. From what I've been told, she'll never give up hope of getting Sacha. The only time she let him slip the leash, he married you, and she's told all her friends that it's just a matter of time before she has him again.'

A matter of time, a matter of time—— The words rang in Katie's ears with the insistence of a buzz saw. Suddenly she was aware that Pat had asked her a question and was waiting for an answer.

'I—I'm sorry. What did you say?'

'This party, Katie. What are you wearing?'

'Oh, you got your invitation, then?'

'Yes. All very formal and correct.'

'*Formal?*'

'Well, elegant, anyway. Engraved on the best linen stationery.'

'That's odd, Pat. It's just supposed to be an informal barbecue.'

'Uh, uh, Katie. I don't know where you got *that* idea, but it's to be a dress-up affair. I understand she's hired a Hawaiian band for music. I think I'll ask Chuck to escort me,' Pat added musingly. 'My ex may think he's God's gift to women, but one thing I *can* say for him, he makes a terribly good impression when he wants to.'

'B-but, Pat, I don't understand,' Katie faltered. 'Claire gave me the definite impression that this was just going to be a small party—a few friends—and I'd expected to wear something casual.'

There was a long silence, then Pat said softly, 'What did she say she was wearing? Or did she?'

'A jumpsuit.'

There was another pause, even lengthier, then, 'Oh, lordy, Katie, there was a jumpsuit in Martelle's window—— If that's the one——' Pat stopped, apparently shocked into stunned silence by the vision of Claire in the Martelle jumpsuit. 'Katie,' she added urgently, 'you'd better get something new to wear to that party—something beautiful! After all, you're the guest of honour, and if it takes every cent you have, honey, you'd better blow it in on an outfit that'll knock her dead!'

When Katie left the phone she was still feeling bewildered by Claire's spite. Reviewing their conversation about the party, she could not remember that the other girl had said anything to make her believe the party was to be a small, casual affair; perhaps it had been the mention of the jumpsuit, but nevertheless, that was the impression that she had been given. And Katie knew that Claire had done it deliberately, hoping that Katie's dress would be hopelessly wrong. But why? The answer was right there—to try to humiliate her and make Sacha's friends pity him for his choice of a wife. And make Sacha reconsider that choice, for of course he would not blame Claire but merely regard it as just another wrong impression of Katie's. He might even think she had done it deliberately in an attempt to embarrass him. Anything was possible after Claire had got through with her poisonous little innuendoes.

It had been nearly a week since their quarrel and things were rapidly going from bad to worse. Yesterday had been the worst yet. All day Sacha had been terribly angry in an icy, civil way, and Katie suspected that Claire had managed to make something of her meeting with Ben, although that would credit Sacha with jealousy—of her. And Katie knew that was impossible. It was more likely that Claire had given him a distorted view of their conversation in the study. For a while Katie had toyed briefly with the idea of going to Ben with the story of Claire's interference, but she knew she couldn't do it. He would be angry—Claire's white face had told her that—and she sensed that he would punish his daughter accordingly. Ben Thorpe would make a bad enemy. Like Sacha. When he looked at her nowadays, she received a chill blast that felt as though it came straight from the North Pole.

She knew that Paul was puzzled by his son's behaviour, and she tried to pretend that all was normal, but last night, by the end of dinner, she was exhausted, her stomach churning with tension. Sacha had left immediately afterwards and she knew now that he was seeing Claire.

Then, this morning, after the conversation with Pat,

Katie made a timid effort to break the deadlock between them.

'Sacha.' She caught him as he was leaving the house, and hated the impatient way he halted.

'Yes?'

'We're going to have to talk. We can't go on like this. It—it's no good.'

'You know what you can do about it.' His face had hardened.

'You mean—crawl?'

His mouth tightened. 'I mean act like a responsible human being for a change. You're right—we do need to talk.' He looked around and dragged her into a small room off the back entrance that was used for flower arranging and odd jobs by Yoshura. He slammed the door shut and then, leaning against the sink, eyed her consideringly. 'Look, Katie,' he began patiently, 'when I met you again, in Honolulu, I was filled with admiration for the job you'd done with yourself and Kim. You'd raised him superbly and made a success of your shop and, according to Pat, even when your aunt died you didn't go to pieces but kept right on struggling. I was even willing to concede you the privilege of waiting until you were ready to consummate our reconciliation.' His mouth twisted with self-derision. 'I thought it was unwise, but I could understand your objections. However, this is different, these sick delusions you're having about Gran and Claire—especially Gran. She's just a sick old lady who loves me! I admit that Claire might tease you some time, but you've no one but yourself to blame for having started the whole thing by showing her you're jealous! Frankly,' he added grimly, 'I don't know if you need a psychiatrist or a marriage counsellor, but personally, I believe the whole thing is nothing more than the irresponsible antics of a spoiled brat!'

Katie stared at him helplessly. It was all so plausible –

and so untrue! But how could she begin to refute it? Didn't he *know* how Claire felt about him?

'You don't think I have a right to resent the fact that you're seeing Claire all the time, more than you're seeing me, then?' she asked stiffly.

'Ask yourself why, some time!' he said savagely. 'For God's sake, Katie, Claire is one of my oldest friends, and one of the dearest. I don't intend to give up her friendship merely because you're unable to handle that fact! Especially,' he added, with deliberate cruelty, 'when she occupies a place in my affections that you could never aspire to. If that's what you're asking, then forget it!'

He wrenched open the door and flung himself out. Katie watched blindly as he took the path to the stables. He was going to find Claire; he was going to tell her everything that had been said and reassure her that he had put his wife firmly in her place. And Katie knew now just what that place was! She shivered and bent over the sink, staring blankly into the mirror that reflected her white face and haunted, tearful eyes.

Suddenly the phone shrilled beside her, startling her so much that she jumped and knocked it off its cradle. Then she had to answer it, as the connection had been opened.

She cleared her throat and picked up the receiver. 'Hello?' she quavered, then repeated it. 'Hello?'

'Katie! Is that you, Katie?'

It was Benjamin Thorpe. Katie hoped that her voice did not sound strange.

'Yes, Ben. How are you?'

'I'm glad you answered. I was hoping you would. Incidentally, I looked for you yesterday while I was riding.'

'L-looked for me?' she asked blankly. 'I—I don't think I walked yesterday.'

'Hey,' he chuckled, 'did I wake you? You sound like you're half asleep. I called to see if you'd like to have that drink with me you promised. This afternoon, about four o'clock, if that's okay with you?'

'This afternoon?' Katie hesitated, then said slowly, 'Would you be able to run me into Honolulu instead, Ben?' He was silent, apparently taken aback by her unexpected request, and she added swiftly, 'If you can't do it, don't worry about it. It's just that I must go today, and if you can't take me, I'll have to go alone.'

'Now, wait a minute—don't be so quick to back out. This sounds interesting. But isn't that a little far to go for a drink?' The smooth, clever voice sounded a little dry.

'Oh, that's not why I asked you to take me.' The thought had burst into her head full-blown, and she spoke without thinking. 'I wanted to go shopping.'

'*Shopping?*' he asked blankly.

'Yes. I need something to wear to your daughter's party. I've just discovered that it's going to be much—er—dressier than she led me to believe, and I haven't a thing to wear. I'll leave it to you to come up with her motive,' she added blandly.

He burst out laughing. He could not only appreciate Claire's motive, but admire her ingenuity. 'Katie my love! This is the first time a woman has put me to use in such an obvious manner since I cut my wisdom teeth. I must say, I can't argue with your honesty. There's only one thing that puzzles me.' His voice dropped suggestively. 'Why me, when you have a husband who has a boat *and* a plane to put at your disposal? However, who am I to question my luck when I seem to be on the side of the angels! When would you like to go?'

'Right away?' she asked tentatively.

'Shall we say in an hour?' Ben countered amusedly. 'I have to arrange for a car and a helicopter. I'm only a visitor in Hawaii, remember? I haven't the amenities of your father-in-law.'

'Oh, Ben, I can't allow you to go to that expense. Forget it! I—I'll find some other way to get there.'

'You wouldn't be so cruel!' he said swiftly. 'Deny me a chance to do you a service? Never! Besides, I have business that I need to attend to in Honolulu, so it's just as well. And if it makes your frugal little soul feel better, we'll plan to return by commercial aircraft. All right?'

'All right,' she said weakly. 'Thanks, Ben. How can I ever repay you?'

'Oh, I'll think of a way,' he said smoothly. 'For starters, what about letting that drink stretch to cover dinner, too?'

Katie dressed carefully for her shopping trip since she planned to wear it to dinner too. She wore a loosely fitting, rather tailored dress of polyester crêpe de chine, with a slit skirt that gave a revealing glimpse of her slim legs. The colour of crushed raspberries, it brought a pinkness to her cheeks and an added sparkle to eyes that, only moments earlier, had been sad and haunted. She was determined to look her best and enjoy herself for a change. What had Ben said? What's sauce for the goose, is sauce for the gander! At the last moment she decided to swirl up her hair, and she hummed as she saw that the style had exposed the fragile gold hoops she wore in her ears.

She found her reward in the look in Ben's eyes when he saw her. I can't help it, she thought defensively, it feels good to know that I look good! To see admiration in a handsome man's eyes. It boosted one's ego, especially when said ego had received quite a battering lately, she added wryly.

They were on their way in to Honolulu in a hired limousine when Ben leaned forward, closing the window between themselves and the driver, then taking her hand, he raised it, palm up, to his mouth.

'Ben,' she said uneasily, trying to detach her hand, 'please!'

'No!' he said sternly. 'Surely you're not going to deny me the pleasure of holding your hand? It's harmless enough, isn't it? What's going on between you and Sacha, Katie?' he added, as she reluctantly abandoned her protests.

'What do you mean?'

'Don't fence with me! How close are you two to breaking point? You're not even communicating enough so that you can ask him to take you to Honolulu! Instead, you're forced to ask a favour of someone whom you might consider a perfect stranger!'

Her heart plunged. 'Are you a perfect stranger, Ben?' She had only wanted to turn him aside from questioning her, but she saw from his swift reaction that she had phrased the question so that it sounded provocative.

'I hope that you don't regard me as one!' he said passionately. 'I don't feel I'm a stranger to you.'

'I'm sorry, Ben,' Katie apologised humbly. 'That was a stupid thing to say. You must think I'm trying to flirt with you.'

'Only a little,' he said quizzically. 'But I meant what I said. I hope you regard me as more than a mere acquaintance. It goes deeper than that with me. As a matter of fact, I think I'm falling in love with you, Katie.'

She flushed. 'Please don't! I don't want to hurt you and I—I—thought you understood what I said the other day. I will *not* become your mistress, Ben.'

'That was a damned fool thing for me to ask you!' he said violently. 'I've been kicking myself for it ever since I left you. I tried to call you a couple of times, meaning to apologise and get us on another footing, but every time, Sacha answered the phone and informed me icily that you weren't available to talk!'

'He—did?' she asked blankly.

'Yes! Damned dog in the manger. He doesn't want you,

but he's determined to hang on to you until he makes up his mind what to do about Claire. He knows she's besotted with him, but she tells me she has to prove herself with the child before he'll have her! Meantime, I'm in love with you, Katie! Thank God you called today, and gave me a chance to tell you. I'm not asking you for anything so damned insulting as an affair—I want to marry you as soon as you're free. I'm serious about this, Katie. I know I'm a poor marriage risk, but this time is different; this time I'm really in love, for the first time in my life,' he protested, almost sulkily, and Katie wondered how many other women had heard precisely those words from Benjamin Thorpe.

'Ben,' she began gently, 'I told you—I'm married. I have a husband, and——'

'And he's leaving you!' he said triumphantly. 'And then you'll be alone, poor darling. I'll wait. Sooner or later, you'll see it for yourself.'

'What makes you say those things?' she demanded.

'Claire.' He said it as though the name explained every-thing. 'I know my daughter too well, my dear. I never have underestimated her determination to get her own way. Perhaps she's like me, but she has her own brand of ruthlessness. She's been possessive about Sacha since she was a child. She turned him against his own mother then, making herself out to be the unwanted stepchild. Even today, Sacha believes Claire to be the victim of selfish, neglectful parents. I came in for my share of villainy, too. That's why Sacha hates me today—that, and my affair with poor old Marjorie. He resented her because she got custody after a bitter court battle with his father. I guess he and Claire united in the face of a common enemy.'

'How old were they?'

'She was nine and Sacha about thirteen. Claire would tell you it's a long time to love one man. I guess she's had her flings—but she always comes back to him, and always will. Even if, by some miracle, your marriage to Sacha survived, you'd always have Claire around his neck.' Katie shivered slightly, as he went on, his voice cynically indifferent as he spoke of his own daughter. 'She was always something of a handful after her mother's death, but I didn't see what was happening until it was too late. By then, she'd turned Sacha against both of us—Marjorie *and* me. Just as she will you, too, Katie. You don't stand a chance. Claire has everything on her side, including the old grandmother—whom Claire will cut out of Sacha's life just as ruthlessly as she will his father or anyone else who stands in the way of what she wants. So—cut your losses, my dear, and give up. You'll only be destroyed if you fight Claire. Sacha trusts her.'

'I can't give up,' Katie said sickly. 'It's not just him. There's—Kim.'

'Oh. The child?' He sounded slightly astonished. 'Does he mean so much to you, then?'

Katie thought it was a measure of how little Ben understood her that he could even ask such a question. 'He does,' she said bleakly.

'Then I might be able to help you there,' he said swiftly. 'I have the money to hire lawyers to fight a custody suit.'

Katie was not such a fool to think he would finance such a suit until she was his wife, but to even talk about it, to admit the possibility, was to make it seem real. 'I'd never fight a bitter court battle over Kim,' she said shrinkingly.

'My poor little innocent, haven't you listened to a word I've been saying?' he demanded roughly. 'Unless Sacha will agree to give Kim up, you'll lose him. Claire will fight tooth and nail to keep the child if that's what it takes to hold Sacha.'

'She's your daughter,' Katie cried despairingly. 'Can't

you control her? Demand that she stop breaking up my marriage?'

Ben's face hardened. 'I want you,' he said brutally. 'I'll use every weapon I have to get you. I won't stop Claire, because if your husband doesn't care enough about you to hold you, then it's better for you to learn it this way right now! He's had two chances with you and he's thrown away both of them. It's my turn, now.'

He pulled her into his arms and planted passionate kisses on her face and mouth. At first Katie struggled, but he was too strong for her and she gradually subsided, until he chose to stop. His kisses hadn't the power to move her, anyway. They meant absolutely nothing. They didn't have the power to blot out for a second the memory of Sacha and what he meant to her. Ben might be an expert lover, but beside Sacha, he was nothing. Finally he released her, and from the look of satisfaction on his face she realised that he had not found anything lacking in her response.

'I'll be back about five, and we'll have dinner before going back to Hawaii,' he murmured caressingly.

She looked up. They had stopped before the shop and the chauffeur was holding the car door open, his face as impassive as a wooden Indian's.

'Ben, I can't have dinner with you if you're going to do this sort of thing——' she began.

'Darling! I promise!' He smiled irresistibly and taking her hand, kissed it lingeringly. 'I'll be strictly impersonal! And you *did* promise!'

'Well, all right.' She crawled reluctantly out of the car. 'Goodbye, then.'

She stood on the kerb, watching the limousine pull away, and thought ruefully that, at times, Ben reminded her of a very spoiled small boy. She did not doubt that he believed himself passionately in love, but his love had an element of selfishness in it that she knew would never find a responsive chord in her own heart. But she wished she could fall in love with Ben. It would be an easy way out. Unfortunately, there was only one man who had the power to turn her bones to water, and that was Sacha.

She turned away from the kerb and noticed the house for the first time. Pat was evidently preparing to have it painted, for it was surrounded by scaffolding, and drop cloths had been draped over the shrubbery. The painters had already begun scraping away the peeling stucco, and it looked garish and ugly. She wondered what Ben had thought when he saw it. In spite of its unattractive appearance, it held the charm of familiarity, and she felt a wave of homesickness for it and the old, uncomplicated life.

Inside, Katie was met by a gum-chewing teenager dressed in her old muu-muu. 'Good morning, moddom. May I help you?' she asked loftily.

'Hello. I'm Katie. I'm looking for Pat.'

'Oh, *yes*, Mrs Kimberly!' the girl gushed. It was obvious that she had picked up some of the gossip that had been circulating all week. 'Pat's in the kitchen.'

The bright, crowded kitchen, flooded by sunlight from the old-fashioned bay window, was reassuringly familiar. The cutting table was still littered with scraps and Pat, sitting at the desk, had the telephone resting on her shoulder as she scribbled on a piece of paper. She looked up and waggled her hand, then grabbed desperately at the slipping phone.

'Be with you in a minute,' she whispered. The business conversation was over in a few minutes and Pat hung up with a relieved sigh. 'Well! This visit is marvellous, although I can't say it's any surprise!' she added impishly.

Just then the phone pealed again and Pat snatched it up with a grimace. 'What? Oh, yes, just walked in.' She looked up, cupping a hand over the mouthpiece, and grimaced again. 'He's been calling every five minutes. What happened? Did you go A.W.O.L.?'

'What? Who?' Katie asked blankly.

'Sacha. Who else? Come on, you can sit at the desk.' Pat handed her the phone and Katie put it gingerly to her ear.

'Hello?' she quavered.

'Katie, what the hell are you playing at?' Sacha sounded furious. 'Is this your idea of a joke or something?'

'I don't know what you mean. Didn't you get—that is, I told Yoshura where I was going.'

'Oh, yes,' he replied savagely, 'I got the message—and the implication. Are you trying to prod me into making some sort of stand?'

'I don't know what you mean,' she repeated dumbly. 'I just came to Honolulu to shop.'

'Then shop!' he said grimly. 'Have it finished by the time I get there!'

'*You* get there?' Katie was astonished. 'You mean you're coming *here*?'

'Naturally,' he said ironically. 'I'll be there in a couple of hours and you be at your place then, waiting for me, or I'll turn Honolulu upside down! I warn you, Katie, don't make me have to look for you!'

Katie hung up the phone and stared at Pat. 'I think Sacha's taken leave of his senses. Why should he mind if I go shopping?'

Pat frowned. 'From what I gathered, the first time he called, it wasn't the shopping so much as who brought you. Who did you come with?'

Katie flushed. 'Oh. Claire's father.'

'Claire's *father*? Why should Sacha mind that?'

'Sacha doesn't like him, although he's been very kind,' Katie said defensively. 'In fact, the way things are going, he may be the only friend I have on Hawaii soon.' She didn't mention Ben's proposal—how could one explain a thing like that? And to Pat? Katie hardly understood it herself. Pawing through the pigeonholes of the desk, she went on rapidly, 'I had him bring me by here so I could get my chequebook. I'm going to take your advice and blow in my savings on an outfit for the party. I'm tired of being taken for a stupid little fool who's everybody's dummy. From here on, I'm through taking insults and sneers, Pat.'

Pat was shocked by Katie's bitterness. On the surface, Katie seemed the same, but there was an underlying note of savage anger that wasn't Katie. Pat had noticed it the moment she walked in. Moreover, she was unhappy and Pat suspected that she had not been getting enough sleep lately.

'Katie, what's the matter?'

Katie kept her face averted as she sifted through the papers on the desk. 'I'm in an awful jam,' she said in a muffled voice.

'Naturally,' Pat said briskly, as though it was the most unsurprising remark in the world. Inwardly, she was appalled. 'Claire Wetherell is a gal who doesn't care what methods she uses to get her man. I wouldn't be surprised if her father isn't the same. Anyway, Sacha doesn't trust him. So—if he's angry with you, just remember it's jealousy speaking, Katie. At least, that's the way he sounded when I talked to him.'

'Oh, no, Pat, he may be angry, but I assure you, he's not jealous!' Katie said bleakly. 'That would mean he cares—and he doesn't. You see, our marriage is over.'

'Katie! Do you know what you're saying?'

'Of course. I'm saying that Claire has won. She's broken up our marriage. I won't go into details about her methods, but they worked. She told Sacha a lie about me, and he believed her.'

'That doesn't sound like the man I met,' Pat said stoutly.

Katie shrugged. 'His grandmother backed her up. She

wants Sacha to marry Claire.'

'Yes, I've heard about her,' Pat mused. 'But, Katie, how can you discuss it so—so calmly? What about Kim?'

A wave of pain crossed Katie's face. 'I'm losing Kim, Pat. Claire told me she would win, and she has. She said she'd take Kim away from me, too, and she's doing it. I can see it happening before my eyes and I can't stop her. She's too clever for me.'

Pat was shaken by a gust of fury. Katie looked desolated. If she had had Sacha Kimberly then, she would have slapped his face on the spot.

'You're going to fight, aren't you?' she demanded.

Katie shrugged wearily. 'I feel like it's a losing battle. If it were just Claire—but Sacha, too——' She dropped her head defeatedly upon her folded arms.

Pat was horrified. 'Katie Lockwood, surely you're going to fight?' she urged. 'You're not going to let that—that man-eater take over your child! As for your—your husband——!' She stopped, too full of the injustice of it to pursue her line of thought about Sacha. As it was, she had to be careful, because Katie looked like being on the brink of a breakdown. She had walked out of here a week ago with stars in her eyes and after just a week, look at her now!

'I've wondered,' Katie replied in a stiff little voice, 'if it wouldn't be better in the end just to fade out of Kim's life. It would only make him confused and unhappy to have his parents living apart, pulling him to pieces between them. Sacha was right about that.'

Pat swore silently. She assumed that this was a recent statement of Sacha's and she was conscious of a strong desire to throttle him. However, it was obvious that Katie was in no mood to be reasoned with, so abruptly she changed the subject. 'Now, see here, we'll talk about this after the party. You're too upset now to make sense. Go on to Martelle's and find yourself something stunning to wear.'

'Something like Claire's?' Katie asked with a wan smile.

'I've been thinking about that jumpsuit, and I know Claire wouldn't wear a thing like that to a big party,' Pat said briskly. 'Now, shoot the works, Katie, shoes, lingerie—the whole thing.'

'I don't have much time. Sacha said he'd be here in an hour or two, and he wanted me through with my shopping by then.'

'Oh, he did, did he?' Pat asked grimly. 'Well, leave Sacha to me. I'll soothe him down if you're late. Have you enough money?'

'I have nearly five hundred dollars in my account,' Katie riffled through her chequebook.

'If that's not enough,' Pat said grandly, 'just let them know who you are. They'll be glad to extend credit.'

It was nearly three hours before Katie returned from her shopping to find Pat waiting on a customer. There was no sign of the gum-popping teenager.

'Did you get something?' Pat asked as soon as they were alone. She eyed the enormous green box tied with gold cord. The name scrawled across its lid in sprawling gold letters was that of a dress shop every bit as famous and expensive as Martelle's.

'Yes. I felt—er—naked in everything I tried on at Martelle's, so I went somewhere else. But you won't be disappointed, I promise you,' Katie smiled slightly. 'Did—did Sacha come?'

'Oh, yes, he came,' Pat said ironically. There was a slight aura of satisfaction about the way she said it. 'He's in the kitchen, using the telephone. Claire's father came, too,' she added suggestively.

'Oh?' Katie stopped. 'What happened?' she asked apprehensively.

'Surprisingly little. Your husband talked to him alone,

but I did hear him say that you wouldn't need him since he was now available to take you home. Mr Thorpe retired gracefully. He's not the type to make a scene or give up easily, either,' she added warningly.

'I suppose not,' Katie said uncomfortably.

Pat grinned mischievously. 'You didn't tell me what a charmer he is. Quite handsome, in fact. He chatted with me a few minutes and before he left, made me promise to save him a dance. I don't know if it was my beautiful eyes or if he was merely trying to get around me because I'm your best friend. He told me that he was looking forward to seeing me at the party.'

Katie smiled wanly. 'So am I,' she said feelingly.

Sacha was putting down the phone, a slight frown on his face, but it smoothed as she walked in. He was dressed for the city, in a cream blazer and slacks that accentuated his dark good looks to a disturbing degree. To Katie's surprise he smiled at her.

Speaking pleasantly, he said, 'Hello, Katie. Finished your shopping? Are you ready to go, then?' He glanced at his watch. 'We're going to have to hurry to make our connections.'

Katie was taken aback. Expecting hostility, she was confused by his politeness. What had happened since this morning? For days he had acted as if he could barely tolerate being in the same room with her and now, suddenly, he was almost friendly. Then a possible explanation occurred. He had talked to Ben and learned that Ben was prepared to take her off his hands. Sacha's geniality stemmed from relief at ridding himself of an unwanted encumbrance! Katie stiffened with indignation at the idea that she was being bartered about like so much merchandise. Sacha was barely hiding his anxiety to be gone and tell Claire about it. Her indignation exploded into anger.

'What's the matter?' she snarled. 'In a hurry to get back to Claire?'

Sacha's expression hardened. 'Cool it, Katie,' he warned. 'I'm in no mood for your bitchiness.'

'Really?' she drawled sweetly, her eyes sending out angry sparks. 'Well, I'm not being hurried off merely to suit your convenience. Why did you bother to come for me, anyway? Ben was going to bring me home, and at least he was giving me dinner first.'

His mouth tightened. 'Yes, you and Ben have got quite friendly lately, haven't you?' he asked grimly. 'That's Ben's speciality—becoming friendly with other men's wives!'

'It's a pleasant change after being treated like dirt all week!' she snapped. 'At least Ben is nice to me.'

'Ben Thorpe is only *nice* when it suits him!' His mocking voice invested the words with sarcasm. 'It wouldn't take much of a brain to understand what all that niceness means—an overwhelming desire to get you into his bed!'

She reddened sharply. 'How can you imply that I——'

'Try to use your head for once, you little fool!' he cut in ruthlessly. 'There are no late flights to Hilo by commercial aircraft, but I bet Ben Thorpe proposed to return that way, didn't he? He would have been very apologetic to learn it, but by then it would have been too late to make other arrangements and there would have been nothing to do but stay in Honolulu overnight at some convenient hotel!' he sneered.

She gulped. 'I don't believe Ben planned anything of the sort!' she declared hotly. 'He's not like you. He hasn't got a mind like a sewer. He's sweet and kind——'

She shrank backwards at the look of naked fury in his eyes.

'Really?' he drawled menacingly. 'It's too bad you're not married to him, then.'

'It's not too late to do something about *that*!'

'And what is that supposed to mean?'

'Exactly what it sounds like! He's asked me to marry him!' she snapped defiantly.

Sacha face changed to a satanic expression that was so terrible Katie cried out in fear, and when he reached for her, she instinctively flinched back, half expecting him to strike her. His lip curled sardonically then, and he gripped her arms with hard, hurting fingers that were so cruelly tight she almost fainted. Then he pulled her into his arms, crushing her breasts painfully against his hard, muscular chest, moulding her slim legs and thighs and soft belly brutally into the rock-like contours of his body. He lowered his head and the hard, cold mouth took hers. It was not a kiss but a ravishment, a hot, fierce exploration of her mouth that was made with only one purpose: to punish, and bring her as quickly as possible to her knees. She could not move, so she did the only thing possible—cling helplessly and seek to accommodate herself to this punishing rape of her senses. She could feel every muscle in his body—indeed, he intended her to feel them—and she wondered dizzily if, when this was over, she wasn't going to be one long bruise from chest to knees.

At last he moved slightly, and her legs buckled. He held her up by the elbows, and spoke through thinned, partially closed lips. 'Listen to me, you stupid little bitch! You're not to open your mouth about Ben Thorpe again! I've never beaten a woman yet, but if I hear another word from you I'll beat you, so help me! Is that understood?'

He shook her roughly and she just managed to gasp, 'Y-yes.'

Just then Pat's head popped in the door. 'Sacha, that taxi you ordered is here.' From the way her head popped out again just as quickly, Katie knew that she had overheard most of their quarrel.

'We're getting out of here!' snarled Sacha. 'So pick up that damned box and *walk*!'

She couldn't walk—Sacha could see that for himself. Muttering an impatient expletive under his breath, he half dragged, half carried her out of the kitchen, through the shop past Pat's astonished face and out into the street where the taxi waited, its motor idling. The driver took one look at Sacha's face and opened the door hurriedly, and Sacha shoved Katie into the cab. She barely had time to scramble out of the way before he was in after her, slamming the door. The explosive directions he flung at the driver sent the taxi spurting away from the kerb in a burst of speed.

'Not only are you never to mention Ben Thorpe's name again, but you're not to accept another invitation, anywhere, from him! I shall tell him tomorrow that he's no longer welcome in my father's home!'

'I——'

'I don't want to listen to any explanations,' he interrupted savagely. 'I mean what I say.'

Katie looked at him warily. She rubbed her arms ruefully, conscious of probable bruises tomorrow, and wondered that she wasn't more shaken than she was. In a strange sort of way she had found Sacha's anger reassuring, but rather than investigate the meaning of that puzzle, she sought to think of something else.

Sacha spoke once, through grimly parted lips, as they were turning off at the airport exit. 'The helicopter was busy, so we're returning by way of commercial aircraft. You'd better do something about your hair.'

He had apparently arranged about their return tickets and they did not have to wait to board the plane for Hilo. As soon as they were seated, Sacha ordered a brandy and soda for himself and a sherry for Katie, without bothering to enquire her preference. After that, he did not speak again, and Katie settled down quietly to endure the flight.

After they had landed Sacha still made no concessions to her, but made his way towards the car park with long strides, leaving her to follow at a half run, carrying her dress box. Finally, in the middle of the strobe-lighted car-park, Katie caught up with him.

'What's the hurry?' she gasped, clutching his arm.

He dropped his eyes coldly to her hand and she flushed and hastily loosened her grip. His eyes were like chips of ice when they met hers.

'There's something wrong at home,' he said coolly. 'The Chief of Police answered the phone when I called.'

She gasped and swayed, and Sacha watched with cruel detachment as she fought to regain control of herself. 'Oh, my God, why didn't you tell me? It's Kim, isn't it? He's hurt—— '

'The Chief said no one had been hurt, but I was to get home as soon as possible, which is just what I intend to do.'

He turned on his heel and continued towards the car, leaving her to follow or stay just where she was, with her legs like rubber and her body almost paralysed with shock.

'You bastard!' she shrilled after him, and she thought he laughed.

By this time he had reached the car, and she saw that he had every intention of leaving her if she didn't hurry. She was frantically clawing at the door as he started the motor, and he leaned over unhurriedly and flicked up the lock. She just managed to fling herself inside as the car started moving.

'Did he say what had happened?' she asked breathlessly.

Sacha didn't answer. In the subdued light from the dashboard, his face looked as though it was carved from stone—and just about as heartless and impervious to shock.

'Damn you, Sacha, answer me!' she half-sobbed.

'Shut up,' he said thinly.

She shut up.

The trip under ordinary circumstances would have taken about an hour, but they made in less than half the time, taking chances that had Katie on the edge of her seat in horror, when she wasn't being flung up against the side of the door. Finally she was moved to remonstrate.

'Sacha, it isn't going to help matters if we kill ourselves——'

He ignored her, but they were at the gate by that time, opening it with a touch of the electronic switch, zooming up the drive, and finally pulling to a stop with a squeal of brakes behind a line of cars, some of which were flashing blue lights.

Katie drew a long, quivering breath. 'Sacha, please,' she begged. 'Wh-what was it?'

'The Police Chief said it was a kidnapping.'

Shock waves went through her. She did not know what she had expected—but not this. A kidnapping meant a child, and there was only one child here—Kim! In spite of her determination not to touch him again, she found herself gripping Sacha's arms with desperate fingers.

'A kidnapping? Oh, my God, it was Kim, wasn't it?'

'I told you he was safe—now.'

She fumbled with the door catch, but her hands were too flaccid to make contact. He got out and opened her door for her, then steadied her as she tried to hurry up the steps.

'Take it easy.'

They were the first sympathetic words he had said to her, but Katie hardly heeded them. They were in the foyer now, and her eyes went frantically to the little knot of people gathered there, uniformed troopers, plain clothes men, and Paul, who was still dressed in the boots and denims he wore while working.

Paul's eyes met hers. 'Katie, don't be frightened . . .'

She pushed past him. Kim was seated on the couch, holding Sammy, and his great-grandmother sat beside him, feeding him ice cream. He was wearing the frayed pair of cut-off jeans that he usually wore while swimming, but someone—no doubt Madam Kimberly—had flung a light fleecy shawl about his shoulders. From the look on his face he was thoroughly basking in the attention he was getting.

'Mommy!' He slid off the couch and Sammy began to leap and bark hysterically. 'Mommy! Something funny happened to Gran'pa and me! A man stole us, but then he let us go! Daddy!' His eyes went past Katie as she lifted him into her arms and buried her face in his thin little neck. 'Daddy, the policeman let me ride in one of the cars with a siren!'

Sacha reached out a convulsive hand that softened to gentleness as he caressed his son's head. With an easy laugh he rumpled the dark, tousled hair. 'Sounds like fun! What happened?' he added in another voice, an altogether different voice, as a powerful-looking man dressed in uniform came into the room.

'Your son and your father were kidnapped this afternoon by a couple of men, Mr Kimberly. It was a bungling attempt—fortunately. Only two men were involved and they were picked up almost at once. They were looking for you, only they accidentally got your son and your father instead, and having no idea what they had, they were talked into releasing them by Mr Kimberly.' A slight smile flitted across the hard features. 'He managed to convince them that he was merely a ranch hand who'd wandered into the house compound looking for the boss, and that the child was his grandson. Dressed as they were, their story was believed.'

'You're all right, Dad?' Sacha's anxious eyes studied Paul's pale, haggard features.

Paul smiled ruefully. 'Now that it's over, it's beginning to hit me, but at the time, thank God, I managed to keep calm enough to talk my way out of it. They'd read that newspaper blurb about you, Sacha, and they were looking for someone to kidnap. If they hadn't been so stupid and ill-informed, it would have been a different story tonight, but when they thought they'd picked up a poor farmer and his grandson, they decided to drop us and avoid a brush with the law. Incidentally, this little mop contributed his share to their capture.' His eyes dropped to Sammy, who was dancing about underfoot, his plumy little tail tightly curled upon his back. 'He followed the car as far as he could, and when the police started to look for us, they were guided by Sammy's barking.'

'A most intelligent little dog,' Madam Kimberly said in her harsh old voice. 'I have always said so.'

Since she had never said anything of the sort, Sacha and Paul burst out laughing, and although no one else knew what the laughter was about, everyone obligingly joined in. There was a general relaxation of tension, and a move was made towards the front door.

'We're leaving a guard on duty tonight and a couple of men tomorrow,' the Chief murmured as he prepared to go. 'Not that I think there's any need. Those two were in it alone and hadn't enough brains between them to plan how to go about it.'

Katie didn't hear him. She had put Kim down, but she was gripping his hand, unaware that Madam Kimberly was watching her closely until she said, 'The boy needs to go to bed, Katie. Would you like Yoshura to see to it?'

'No,' gasped Katie, looking blindly at Madam Kimberly. 'No, thank you,' she added politely, but still rather blankly.

She met Sacha in the doorway and he stood aside and watched until she went through. The eyes that followed her were unreadable, as he watched her mount the stairs, leading Kim.

'What do you plan to do about this, Sacha?' His grandmother sounded fearful.

'I think you know what I must do, Gran.' He hadn't taken his eyes off Katie. 'She isn't used to our kind of life. I'm afraid I forgot that for a while. She didn't expect this when she came here.'

Much later, Katie was awakened by Sacha. She was still sitting beside Kim's bed, cramped and stiff and fully dressed, with Sammy curled up asleep in her lap.

'Time to get in bed, Katie.' His voice sounded strained. 'You slept through dinner. Are you hungry?'

She sat up groggily, rubbing her eyes, puzzled by the oddness in his voice. 'I'm so tired,' she murmured, clinging helplessly as he pulled her to her feet.

'I know.' He bent and lifted her into his arms and carried her to her bed. 'Do you want something to eat?'

'I just want to go to sleep.' His face was so close she could see the bruised lines of strain under his eyes. Now that she was awakening, she knew that she did not want to sleep and she certainly did not want Sacha to take away the security of his arms. 'Don't leave me,' she whispered, clinging to his neck, her mouth brushing his cheekbones. He lowered her to the bed, but her weight caused him to lose his balance and he toppled forward, half falling across her.

'Katie,' he groaned. His hands cupped her yielding breasts, then reluctantly he opened her dress to his exploring fingers. 'Katie, you don't know what you're saying——'

'Stay with me,' she begged. 'Please, darling——'

Sacha murmured something as he buried his face in the

heated valley between her breasts, and breathed deeply the perfume from her body Her body arched, following the line of his lips, and she moaned softly below her breath.

'Katie, this is madness,' he cried hoarsely. 'I can't stay with you. You—don't know what you're asking.'

She opened her eyes. The room was wheeling in a slow, dizzying spiral that was gradually, ever so easily, increasing its tempo. As his words penetrated her consciousness, the spiral came to a swift, merciless halt. She raised her head slightly.

'Wh-what?'

He raised a tormented face. 'Katie, you're tired and scared. You don't know what you're saying. I can't stay with you.'

She sat up suddenly, clawing her way out of his relaxed grip. A deep blush suffused her face. She remembered that he had once predicted this—that she would beg him. She wanted to scream and hide her mortified face from his eyes.

'I know what I'm saying now,' she said shakily. 'And you're right—you can't stay with me. P-please go.'

'Katie, sweetheart——'

She wouldn't meet his eyes.

'Please, Sacha, just go.' Her face was closed in a stubborn little mask.

She felt him hesitate, then he gave a deep sigh and stood up.

'Yes, of course.' His voice was bleak. 'I came in to ask you to get some rest tonight. We'll be making an early start tomorrow.'

She nodded indifferently, not having the slightest idea what he was talking about. He waited, apparently expecting her to question him, and when she didn't he added coolly, 'That's that, then. Goodnight.'

Katie waited, holding her breath until the door closed, scared even then to let it and herself go until she was sure he would not be returning. Finally, after a long suffocating minute, she jumped up and ran to the door and locked it. Then and then only she allowed herself to give way to the racking sobs that tore her slim body until at last, from sheer exhaustion, she slept.

CHAPTER EIGHT

THE following morning by nine o'clock, Katie was on her way to Kauai with Sacha and a laconic, tobacco-chewing cowboy, who seemed as much at home behind the controls of the helicopter he was piloting as he would have been astride a horse.

Kauai—the Garden Island, the green, green island. Here, legend said, the rainbow was born on an island whose origins were lost in a mist of time as vaporous as the mists that circled its highest mountain peak. Here the little people, the *menehune*, lived, and here the fire goddess, the legendary Pele, was born so that she could put the fires in the volcanoes that dotted the Hawaiian landscape.

Since coming to Hawaii, Katie had been fascinated with the stories of Kauai and with the idea of seeing it, but not like this, and certainly without Kim. After the kidnapping and Sacha's rejection of her last night, she had been shocked that he would expect her to leave Kim and take off with him on some unexplained wild goose chase. There had been a stormy hour until Katie's hysterics had to be subdued by force. Sacha had pointed out that the ranch was crawling with guards, and when Katie saw them through the window, patrolling the grounds with guns strapped to their hips, she had screamed that her child was not going to live like this, like a prisoner in an armed camp.

He had slapped her face then, and when she burst into loud, gasping sobs, she realised that she had been on the brink of hysteria.

When she had calmed down, she taunted him with Claire's party.

'What if something happens and we can't get home

tonight? Have you thought about what your precious Claire will think if you miss her party? Are you sure you want to take a chance on making your lover angry with you?'

A brief, ugly look crossed his face. 'Shut up, Katie,' he said coldly. 'If you're trying to rile me into staying at home, forget it! So we miss the party. It won't be the first, or the last, I'll miss. Don't tell me you're upset about that? I thought you weren't anxious to go anyway?' he added mockingly.

'And why are you so anxious to go to Kauai?' she demanded.

'I thought you'd never ask,' he replied ironically. 'I'll tell you in the helicopter.'

The trip to Kauai was short and direct, veering in a north-easterly direction and passing the other islands on their right. The first land they sighted was one of Kauai's mountain-locked beaches. Katie, who was getting to be a seasoned air traveller, was gazing raptly when Sacha's voice suddenly spoke in her ear.

'Do you know anything about Kauai?'

It was their first exchange since leaving the house, and Katie briefly considered maintaining a dignified silence, but her natural curiosity could not allow her to forgo an opportunity to learn more about the state in which she lived. After all, she would only be cutting off her nose to spite her face. She shook her head stiffly.

'No? Well, it's our oldest island, according to the geologists, and the first one discovered by Captain Cook on his voyage of 1778. It's been largely left in its natural state, partly because of the difficulty in building roads and partly through the determination of the planning fathers to keep it from becoming commercialised and exploited. So you can see it's the nearest thing we have in the islands to what Hawaii was once like. At one time Kauai was covered with big sugar cane plantations, but most of them have been broken up into small farms. You can see if you'll look out. I've asked Joe to take us for a little air tour of the island.'

Katie stirred restively. Sacha was close, entirely too close, and when he leaned forward to point out something, he rested his other hand lightly and possessively on her shoulder.

Just then the helicopter tilted and seemed to swerve, and what had been flat canefields below became mountain slopes threaded with rivers that began as waterfalls high on their misty peaks.

'Waialeale,' Sacha told her. 'The rainiest spot on earth. And there's the Alahi Swamp. It's a bonanza for botanists and bird lovers.'

The scene changed then to a cruel-looking gorge, its chiselled rock-bound sides bitten deeply by a narrow, twisting river that lost itself among the crevasses. Katie shivered slightly.

'That's Waimea Canyon,' Sacha explained. 'It could be called a hunter's paradise, because it abounds with wild boar, pheasants, and mountain goats. They're about the only life form that can climb the walls of the canyon.' He laughed. He had apparently regained his good humour. Either he had forgotten their quarrel or the stunning scenery had worked a miracle.

'This island has everything,' he went on, relaxing indolently in his seat. 'If you want the tropical paradise of a Florida, the mountains and canyons of a Colorado, or even the deserts of the Southwest, you've got it all right here, on Kauai. And for sheer, breathtaking beauty, there's nothing to equal Na Pali.'

'Na Pali?'

He pointed, and Katie gasped. Joe had saved the most spectacular view for the last. Beneath her was a rugged coastline of valleys and cliffs that formed jagged ramparts above the sea. From the air, the cliffs were stark, bare and wrinkled, while in the crevasses, like black shadows, were the lush valleys where the early Hawaiians lived. There was a mist hanging over it all that gave the area a dawn of creation look that made Katie shiver slightly with superstitious fear. Seeing it like this, it was easy to believe in the old legends.

The helicopter bore inland, throwing its shadow before the sun, and Katie came abruptly out of the past into the very real present. So far, nothing that Sacha had said explained this sudden, inexplicable trip.

Beside her he stirred, tightening the seat belt he had loosened in order to lean forward.

'Katie.'

By sheer effort of will, he was making her look at him. She turned reluctantly, seeing him, really seeing him, for the first time today. He had ordered her to dress for hiking, and he himself was wearing jeans and a pair of work-manlike brogues. He carried a dacron windbreaker and one of her sweaters in his lap. He grinned mockingly, drawing her eyes to his face, and she noticed that the black lashes resting on his cheekbones were like Kim's when he, too, grinned. There were faint bruises beneath his eyes, as though he hadn't slept well, and he was watching her with an oddly speculative look in their depths that brought back a vivid recollection of how she had begged him to stay with her the night before. Somehow she knew he was thinking of the same thing. Reddening, she raised haughty eyebrows. 'Well?'

'I guess you're wondering why we've come here?' Sacha asked quizzically.

'It had occurred to me,' she said coolly, her shuttered face giving nothing away.

'This is where I intend to live. Down there.' He jerked his head. 'On Kauai.'

Katie was dumbfounded. Whatever harebrained reason

Sacha had for dragging her away like this, today—of all days!—she had certainly never expected this. Live here on Kauai, and not with his father! For heaven's sake, she wondered, did his grandmother know about this?

'You see,' he explained, 'a lot of that land down there used to be Tillotson land. Before he died, my grandfather sold all the cane mills and parcelled most of the land off into farms so that it could be bought in smallholdings. There were a number of reasons, but mostly the growing of sugar cane was no longer so profitable. My uncle Oscar retained part of the land, about five thousand acres, for a cattle spread. He lives there now with my aunt Ellie—they have no children—and he runs about two thousand head of cattle on his spread.'

'Like your father?'

'Yes, but with a difference. Uncle Oscar has always kept a low profile. I doubt if many of his neighbours think of him as having money. Unlike Father, he's never received a glare of publicity from Mother's—er—exploits.' His lips twisted derisively. 'My mother thrives on publicity. She's a press agent's dream—her marriages, her divorces, the whole jet set thing. And each time my father gets the backlash.'

And so do you, Katie thought with a flash of perception. And how you hate it! All those mixed-up feelings of love and hate towards your mother must have been painful to live with.

'That's why I'm getting out, until things quiet down. My uncle bought me some beachfront land, and I'm building a house on it. That's where I intend to raise Kim.'

Katie had been listening carefully, but she hadn't heard him say anything about her. Once she would have assumed it, but not now, not after this past mixed-up ten days, and especially not after last night.

By now the helicopter was hovering over the airfield,

before setting down with such a minimum of fuss and jarring that Katie knew Joe was a very good pilot indeed. As the blades revolved slowly to a clattering stop, Joe pushed the baseball cap he was wearing farther back on his head and unwound his lanky frame from the cramped position behind the pilot's seat. Taking careful aim with his tobacco juice out the open door, he drawled, 'Any idea just when you'll be goin' back, Sacha?'

'No. Some time late this afternoon.'

'We-ell, no sweat.' Joe aimed and spat again. 'I'll be hangin' around here when you're ready to go.'

Sacha crawled out of the door, then held up his arms to help Katie down. In her jeans and shirt, she felt self-conscious, but no one seemed to be paying any attention to them.

Sacha put a casual hand under her elbow. 'Look around for a jeep,' he suggested.

Which was ridiculous, since the car park was full of jeeps. Nothing less would navigate some of these roads. Suddenly, before they had taken more than a few steps, Sacha was roughly seized from behind with a wild whoop that rang in their ears, and Katie looked around in time to see him smothered in a bear hug by a huge, barrel-chested man wearing cowboy boots and khakis. His sandy hair was liberally sprinkled with grey and the weathered brown face over Sacha's shoulder was split by an enormous grin.

'Oscar!' Sacha disengaged himself long enough to get his breath before Oscar began to pound him on the back. 'Oscar, you old scoundrel! It's good to see you.'

'I've been waiting for this day for a long time!' Oscar bellowed in what he probably thought was a normal conversational tone.

'Oscar, this is Katie——'

'No need to introduce us. I know who the little filly is!' He seized her in a bone-crushing hug, then gave her a smacking kiss. Katie, slightly taken aback, looked up into a pair of kindly eyes beaming at her from one of the homeliest faces she had ever seen.

'I hope I haven't scared you, honey. How long has it been since I've seen you, boy? Katie, he used to be one of my best wranglers when he was just a shirt-tail kid. I sure hated to lose him, when he decided to leave me and go to the big city and learn how to paint pretty pictures.'

The drawl was straight Texas. So was the battered Stetson and the slightly bowed legs in faded khaki. He looked like a broken-down cowboy beside Sacha, who even in jeans and open shirt projected an air of casual elegance.

Suddenly Oscar chuckled. 'This little gal's wondering if I'm really your uncle. Guess we're nothing alike. But I'm his maw's brother, and if you're finding that hard to believe, wait until you meet Marjorie. She's a first-class beauty and you'll wonder how an ugly mutt like me can have such a gorgeous sister. Say, Buddy!' the affectionate nickname made Katie's eyes widen, 'where's your little 'un? I thought you'd bring him with you.'

'We left him with my father. I wanted Katie to see the site today. Another time we'll bring him.'

'Well, okay, but Ellie's going to be mighty disappointed.'

By this time Oscar was leading the way to the waiting jeep. He heaved some farm machinery and bags of dog food into the back to clear a place for Sacha, and Katie was obliged to sit on her husband's lap. Oscar climbed in behind the wheel and started the engine, then went out of the parking lot on two wheels. Katie, wedged into place by a saddle that was digging a hole in her knee, clutched a handful of Sacha's shirt in a terrified attempt to keep her balance just as Oscar careened into the traffic, still on two wheels, and just ahead of an indignant motorist. He was forced to slow down then, to conform to the traffic, but he talked with his hands off the steering wheel, and only returned them when it became necessary to avoid an oncoming car.

Lihue was a town of balconied, two-storey frame houses reminiscent of the old West in the good old days. Oscar should feel right at home here, Katie thought ironically, as they breezed through town running the two traffic lights, while Oscar bellowed greetings to people whom he knew. By now Katie was frankly clinging to Sacha for dear life.

When they were ready to turn off, Oscar had to slow long enough to put the jeep into second gear, but when he turned into another road he increased speed until he pulled up to a screeching halt, before a gate. Katie got out shakily to open it, and suggested that she walk the rest of the way, but Oscar was having none of that.

'Hurry up, girl, they're waiting for us!' he hooted.

Sacha was shaking with laughter as he pulled her up into his arms, and she darted him a murderous look.

'Shall I open the next gate?' he breathed in her ear.

But the next gate was opened by a cowboy mounted on a horse, and he gave them a mocking salute as they barrelled through before finally pulling to a bone-rattling halt before the house.

It was a big, two-storey house that looked as though it had begun life during the gingerbread Victorian era of houses. It bore no relationship to the modern Kimberly mansion. Built of weathered wood, with both a porch and a balcony, it was partially overshadowed by a flowering bougainvillea vine. Other flowers, as lavish and lush as though they had flourished naturally from seed were in full bloom among the many trees that filled the lawn.

Oscar sounded his horn with a flourish, and Katie gingerly began to move her arms and legs.

'By the way, Sacha,' Oscar began with a faintly embarrassed air, 'I should have told you——'

He got no farther. The front door opened and about six bird dogs flew out and down the steps, baying, their tails streaming, followed by a pretty little brown-haired woman whose arms were outstretched.

'Sacha!' she screamed, and flung herself into his arms.

He laughed and swung her up so that he could kiss her. 'Ellie!'

Oscar was pounding both their backs. 'Leave go, woman! He has someone with him you want to meet.'

'Oh?' Ellie peered shyly at Katie over Sacha's shoulder.

Suddenly Sacha stiffened, then put his aunt down carefully with a curiously rigid gesture. Katie glanced at him curiously, then followed the direction of his eyes to the front door. Framed in it was a tall, slim woman with a mop of flaming red hair and one of the most beautiful faces Katie had ever seen. Her breathtaking figure was sheathed in a pair of tightly fitting white slacks and a soft chiffon blouse with a scoop neckline. From here, she looked a possible forty, although Katie knew she was fifty-four. She recognised her at once, having seen her face on Paul's dresser, plus innumerable candid shots in papers and magazines. Marjorie Tillotson. Sacha's mother.

Marjorie slowly descended the steps of the old-fashioned porch, and as she emerged into the glaring sunlight Katie could see that the illusion of youth had been fostered by distance. There were fine lines around her mouth and the haunting green eyes wore a look of weary cynicism.

'That's what I was trying to tell you, Buddy. I—we—called Marjorie when we heard about the boy,' Oscar said apologetically.

'And why shouldn't we?' Ellie demanded defiantly. 'She's the child's grandmother, isn't she?'

Marjorie cleared her throat nervously. 'I—you don't mind, do you, Sacha?' she pleaded.

Staring from one to the other, Katie was shocked to

realize that these three people were afraid of Sacha's reaction to what they had done. They were waiting with bated breath for that handsome, expressionless face to change, either to anger or at the very best, tolerance. He frowned slightly, and she willed him not to hurt them. Slowly the taut lines of his face relaxed.

'Of course not, Mother,' he said smoothly. 'I'm glad to see you.'

Marjorie's face lighted and she came forward swiftly. 'Darling, thank you,' she said huskily, embracing him.

Somewhere beneath that carefully cultivated accent was a hint of Oscar's Texas drawl, but it was concealed beneath layers of sophistication. In spite of her age, too, she was glamorous in a way that made Claire seem phoney and adolescent.

Sacha introduced Katie and Marjorie hugged her convulsively. To her surprise, Katie found herself warming to this chic, beautiful woman. She had not expected to, but who could help liking someone who seemed almost pathetically glad to meet her?

'Marjorie was afraid for us to let you know she was here,' Ellie explained. 'She was afraid you'd cancel your trip if you knew.'

'I wouldn't do that,' Sacha replied.

With a whoop of exultation Oscar flung his arm around Katie's shoulders and led the way into the house. The living room, or parlour, as Oscar called it, was a big panelled room with a huge rock fireplace at one end. It was furnished mostly with Victorian antiques, but a scrambled collection of oddities from Hawaiian artifacts and scrimshaw to Waterford crystal and Chinese blue jostled each other on the shelves, tables and mantel.

'Now everyone sit down and chat while I get on with dinner,' Ellie said briskly, whipping out an apron and tying it around her waist.

'No cook, Ellie?' Sacha questioned, his eyes gleaming with amusement as he eyed the little martinet figure.

'No one can cook as well as *I* can, especially when it comes to a company dinner!' she boasted, and bustled out to the kitchen.

Oscar laughed. 'The truth is she doesn't want another woman in her kitchen,' he teased, and she paused long enough to say, threateningly, 'Just you wait, Oscar Tillotson!'

It was apparently an old exchange between them, and Oscar's eyes held a gleam of anticipation as he watched her retreating back. He turned to Katie when she had gone, and suggested that he show her around the house. She realised that his real purpose was to leave Sacha and Marjorie alone for a while.

'Guess you're wondering how a big bear of a fellow like me was able to persuade that pretty little thing to marry me?' he queried as they were finishing their tour of inspection.

'Well, I——'

'I'll tell you how it happened. You see, my gran'pa came out here in the 90's from Texas and struck it rich growing sugar cane and pineapples. Sent back to Texas for his bride and sent his son back there for his education and *his* bride, too,' Oscar drawled, his eyes twinkling as they met hers. 'We Tillotson men always went in for spunky little women and football. When it came my time, I played ball for Texas and found Ellie sitting over there in the girls' dormitory, just waiting for me. When Pa got out of the sugar business, lock, stock and barrel, he invested in gilt-edged stocks. It began to look like I wasn't going to have a danged thing to do all day but sit around and clip coupons. I knew a few years of *that* and I'd get so mean and bored that Ellie would leave me, so I finally figured out I'd better find something to do quick to keep myself busy. And there wasn't anything I wanted to do more than raise cattle, so here I am.'

'And the coupons?'

'Oh, they get clipped.' The drawl intensified. 'And occasionally I use my money to buy something I want. Like a couple of hundred acres of prime beach property I bought for Sacha when I learned he wanted to come back here to live and work. It's waiting for you and that little kid of yours, Katie, and a dream house is going up on it. With its windows looking towards the sea and nothing between you and the whole Pacific Ocean. You know, Katie,' he added, as he led her through the old-fashioned entry hall, 'a man isn't worth much unless he's doing the work he likes. It's the same with a woman. I guess that's what's been wrong with Marjorie all this time. She's a Tillotson, and she's just plain going against her nature.'

'Ellie doesn't regret having a chance to live the same sort of life as Marjorie?' Katie quizzed smilingly.

'Ellie?' His eyebrows raised comically. 'Good lord, no! You just ask her for yourself. Come on.'

He led the way to the kitchen, and Katie saw that he just wanted an excuse to put his hands on his wife. Ellie was flitting between the sink and the stove, and he came up behind her and wrapped his arms around her so that she couldn't move.

'I'm busy, Oscar Tillotson,' Ellie said automatically, but she did not seem to be in any hurry to prove it.

'You think you're going to enjoy having Katie as your neighbour?' he murmured, pressing a kiss into the back of her neck.

'I'm just thankful Sacha found Katie again before he was tempted to take up with that snooty Claire Thorpe!' Ellie said tartly. 'That would have really put the fat in the fire so far as I'm concerned! I can take a lot of things, but having that one around me, day in and day out, would have been too much.'

Oscar chuckled. 'You women always have your knife in poor Claire. I think she's mighty pretty myself,' he teased.

Ellie sniffed. 'Pretty is as pretty does.' She pushed him away. 'Just go on out to the barn or somewhere and keep busy till you're called. It seems to me that's about all you're good for.'

He paused in the doorway. 'She's mad because I didn't agree with her about Claire,' he laughed, winking at Katie.

'Men!' Ellie sniffed as the door closed behind him. Her cheeks were flushed and Oscar's nuzzling had disarranged the soft, fluffy hair.

'All right, Katie, what's this all about?' she demanded sternly. 'I happened to be looking at you when I mentioned Claire Thorpe. What's wrong?'

'Nothing,' Katie said weakly. 'I just don't like her, either.'

'Uh, uh, it's more than that. You've been real sweet and said all the right things so far, but I've got a feeling that there's something wrong.'

'Ellie,' Katie began uncertainly, 'I hate for you and Oscar to plan—to count on me as your neighbour. I—I think you'd better know there's a good chance I won't be living with Sacha in that new house Oscar was talking about.'

Ellie looked stunned. 'What on earth are you trying to say?'

'I'm trying to explain.' Katie swallowed convulsively. 'His—Sacha's—loyalties are d-divided. Right now, it's sort of up in the air.'

'Up in the air?' Ellie screeched, then lowered her voice hastily. 'How can it be up in the air? You're his wife, aren't you?'

'I wouldn't have said anything,' Katie admitted miserably, 'but you've been so nice and—you see, I guess you don't know that Sacha and I recently met again after all this time. Five years——'

'I know all that,' Ellie said calmly. 'He called and told us the whole story. That's when we called Marjorie.'

'Oh.' Katie's eyes wavered and she gulped and started again. 'Then you probably know that he and Claire were engaged until I came back into his life.'

'I don't know anything of the sort!' Ellie objected. 'Sacha never told me that. But if he'd wanted to marry Claire, he had plenty of time, didn't he? You and he have been separated long enough.'

'Separated, but not legally divorced——'

Ellie was regarding her impatiently. 'So what? A divorce is easily got—for desertion, if nothing else,' she added sarcastically. 'And where did you get all this stuff about him wanting to marry Claire? Did Sacha tell you that?'

'No-o-o,' Katie stammered. 'Claire told me—and Madam Kimberly.'

'Oh, that one!' Ellie sniffed. 'I'd suspect anything she said. Claire set out from the beginning to win her and Paul over and she succeeded—with the old Madam. But it only lasted with Paul until he caught on that her pretty little ways hid a mean spirit. She never did try it with Oscar and me, although she used to follow Sacha over here often enough, goodness knows! But we're Marjorie's family, and of course, she's always hated Marjorie.'

'Yes, I know,' Katie muttered.

'Ha! Who told you?' Ellie pounced quickly.

'Ben. Benjamin Thorpe.'

'He's there, too?' A trace of amusement flickered across Ellie's face. 'It sounds like we're going to have you and Sacha as our neighbours quicker than we expected. No wonder Sacha wants to hurry the workmen up!'

'He does?' Katie asked blankly.

'Sure he does. He's anxious to get that house finished.

Listen here, Katie. I don't know what kind of muddle you've dreamed up, but so far as I can tell, it all boils down to one thing. Do you love Sacha?'

'Yes.'

'Well then, tell him so. You're his wife; the child is your son. And his. I can't see where you've a thing to worry about.'

It did seem simple, from Ellie's point of view, but before Katie could open her mouth and try to explain just how complicated it was, Marjorie came into the room. From the evidence of her slightly reddened eyelids, Katie suspected that she had been crying.

'I'm going back in the helicopter with you,' she said huskily to Katie. 'Sacha suggested it might be the best thing to do. Then I can see Kim tonight and be able to leave tomorrow.'

'Tomorrow?' Ellie gasped. 'But you've just got here!'

'Oh, I know, but it's all a drag, really,' Marjorie drawled in a bored voice. 'Anyway, Sonny Montford is organising a yachting party for the fifteenth, and I have to get back to California and get something decent to wear.'

'Marjorie Tillotson, shut up and sit down!' Ellie stood over her, glaring. 'You know very well you came here prepared to stay until your latest divorce is final, and longer if necessary! For once, why don't you think of someone besides yourself? Katie's in trouble,' she added, with ominous calm.

Marjorie's eyes flew to Katie. 'Trouble?'

'Oh, I don't really think——'

'Yes. Claire Thorpe!'

Marjorie's face hardened and Katie saw that her mother-in-law could make a bad enemy. She might not be malicious, but when it came to ruthlessness, she would return tit for tat. In that, Sacha was more like his mother than he knew.

'So she's still in the picture?' she mused scornfully. Her eyes considered Katie thoughtfully. 'And you haven't a clue as to how to beat her, have you? What does Sacha say about it?'

'I—I think Sacha will soon be asking me for a divorce so that he can marry Claire,' Katie confessed reluctantly. She was secretly appalled at what was happening. How in the world had she got into this discussion? Ordinarily reticent about her affairs, here she was, blabbing the whole business to two utter strangers! 'I'm sure you don't want to hear all this,' she added weakly.

Ellie gave that statement the contemptuous silence it deserved. Marjorie, fitting a cigarette into her long holder, merely said impatiently, 'Go ahead.'

Unwillingly Katie complied, and when she had finished, Marjorie and Ellie exchanged a long look.

'It sounds like you could use some help,' Marjorie said reflectively. 'If it were just Claire, I'd say you have nothing to worry about until Sacha tells you himself. But apparently she has his grandmother on her side, and my ex-mother-in-law is another matter. If she wants this, she's dangerous. You haven't told Sacha any of this?'

'No!' Katie blew her nose fiercely. 'Do you think he'd believe me?'

'Probably not,' Marjorie agreed calmly. 'He adores his grandmother—almost as much as he dislikes me. Well, that settles it,' she added abruptly. 'It's time Claire Thorpe and I had it out. She ruined my relationship with my son, and because she was only a child I couldn't fight her. She had all the advantages on her side, and boy, did she use them!' She laughed mirthlessly. 'But we're both adults now, and it's time we met with the gloves off.'

There was a sound of male laughter outside, and Ellie rose at once and, opening the oven door, began to check the doneness of the potatoes surrounding the roast.

'Ellie, why don't you get Oscar to modernise this kitchen for you?' Marjorie asked impatiently. 'At the very least, get a microwave oven?'

'What's wrong with my kitchen?' Ellie was demanding just as Oscar walked in with Sacha. 'I like it the way it is.'

The house was a dream. Situated in splendid isolation, surrounded by a thick tropical growth of trees, it was located on a cliff top that overlooked the sea. The private beach below was gained by way of a set of rough steps that had been built into the side of the cliff. Sacha had borrowed Oscar's jeep to get to the house, following a rutted logging road that had been used by the trucks carrying supplies to the site.

The workmen had taken off for the rest of the day, and when Katie crawled out of the jeep and stood looking at the house, she was greeted by a profound silence, broken only by the sound of birds and the distant roar of the surf. The house looked exciting, even from the outside. It had gone beyond a floor and framework; it had walls, a roof, even rooms and open windows. As Katie followed Sacha through the empty, echoing rooms, sniffing the unmistakable odour of raw lumber, she could visualise the way it would look some day. It was a house that one could be happy in; a beautiful house, designed for living. In spite of its isolation, she could find no flaw: it was accessible to schools and the big city life of Honolulu was no farther than the airport. Not that Katie had any hankering to return to *that*. And she would have Ellie and Oscar for neighbours——

But Sacha said nothing about who was going to live in the house with him. In the kitchen they paused while he pointed to where he intended to build a garage, with an apartment above it for a couple, a gardener and possibly a cook or a housemaid. Suddenly Katie couldn't stand it any more—the ambiguity, the uncertainty of *not knowing*.

She lashed out frustratedly.

'I don't know if it will work out with Kim,' she snapped pettishly. At the same time, she was horrified by what she was saying. 'I intend to have his custody part of the time, and I'm not sure I like the idea of shuttling him back and forth between Kauai and Honolulu all the time.'

Sacha's face darkened.

'Really?' he drawled icily. 'Surely you would be willing—for Kim's sake—to put up some sort of little shop in Lihue so you could see him once in a while?'

She gasped, hurt, yet striking back wildly in a primitive urge to conceal her wound from his coldly probing eyes.

'Go to hell!'

She could feel the tears coming and she turned and fled blindly, just as they gushed out of her eyes and rolled down her cheeks.

'Where are you going?' he demanded.

'Anywhere—away from you,' she screamed hoarsely.

'Katie, come back here!'

He caught up with her as she was trying desperately to turn on the ignition key. Snatching it out of her hand, he flung it on the floor of the jeep and at the same time yanked her out of her seat. By that time she was frankly bawling, and he was momentarily taken off balance at the sight of her streaming eyes. She took advantage of it by rushing him with clawing nails, and screaming fury.

'Oh, no, you don't, you little hellcat!' He clasped her flying wrists in a paralysing grip, while with the other hand he yanked her head roughly back. 'Why are you crying?'

For answer, she jerked her head forward and bit his shoulder.

'Damn!' He was angry now. 'You've been asking for this! Today, for a change, you're going to grow up!' he promised grimly.

He started towards the house at a rapid pace, dragging her behind him. She was half running, going too fast to bite or kick, or any of the things she might normally have done. Once she lifted her hands to bite his wrist, but the movement with which he warded off her attack smashed her mouth against her teeth, numbing it with pain. At the steps she fell, bumping her knees, but Sacha didn't pause when she cried out.

In the kitchen, he stopped and faced her, and she saw that he was in a flaming temper, his face a white mask of fury. 'I think,' he said harshly, 'that the bedroom would be the appropriate place, don't you?' And with a single fluid movement he bent and tossed her over his shoulder.

She screamed as enlightenment struck her, and began to pound on his back with her fists.

'You devil! Let me go!'

She fell to the floor fighting, but he restrained her easily by the simple method of rolling over and holding her body down with his weight. Her wrists were captured, twisted and pinned above her head, and her hair was caught tautly beneath his elbow so that she couldn't move. Tears of pain sprang into her eyes and rolled down her cheeks, but she met his hard, unsmiling eyes defiantly.

Deliberately, at his ease, Sacha unbuttoned her shirt and bra, baring her body to his possessive eyes. Katie writhed and bucked as, with torturous slowness, his free hand cupped one of her breasts, his thumb beginning a sensitive rotating movement that wrung a hoarse cry from her lips. He studied her almost curiously, then lowered his hard, cold mouth to hers and took her lips. From that moment she was lost. From being an unwilling prisoner she had become a willing captive. He sensed her surrender, and his lips softened as he explored her hot, moist mouth, then trailed fiery kisses from the tender curve of her cheekbones to her damp, tear-stained eyelids, before pausing to breathe deeply the sweet smelling perfume of her hair. He released her hands and unconsciously they sought his head, as the slim fingers burrowed deeply into the thick black hair. His mouth wandered tenderly to her breasts, pausing to kiss one rose-tipped peak before her soft moans forced him to seek hungrily for her mouth again.

At some period of time he had removed her jeans, and now he guided her body gently beneath his own, filling her with such a shock of pleasure that she rose beneath him, his name an inarticulate cry on her lips. She clung to him, her body racked with tremors of rapturous bliss, her loins aching with the need to find fulfilment. Her body heated, and suffused her cheeks with a glow of colour. She opened her glazed, passion-filled eyes and saw his face above her, dark, intense, rigid.

'I love you, Sacha,' she breathed, then gripped his back, feeling the hardened, bunched muscles beneath her clutching fingers as the dizzying spiral increased in tempo.

Gradually the shivers subsided, and Katie lay limply in his arms. Raising himself upon his elbows, he framed her face with his palms and softly kissed her trembling mouth, then sank back upon the hard floor with a sigh.

Katie rolled over and buried her face in her hands. She was desperately ashamed of the ease with which Sacha had gained her willing co-operation. Would he remember what she had said? Had she lowered the last bastion in her defence against him? She could only wait dumbly, for whatever he chose to say or do.

It came soon enough.

Rolling her into his arms, he bent over her smilingly.

'Come on, baby,' he commanded deeply. 'Playtime's over. Get up and get dressed. I don't want to miss Claire's party.'

CHAPTER NINE

'BUT I miss-ted you, Mummy, I miss-ted you! An' Sammy miss-ted Dad-dy! You should've waked me up so I could go, too.'

'I'm sorry, darling.' Katie bent over and kissed the dark curls as she struggled to thrust the wriggling little body into pyjamas. 'We had to go, but we've come back. And next time, Daddy says he'll take you with him. And Sammy, too,' she added hastily. 'Did you have a lesson today, or was Claire too busy with her party?' she added diffidently.

'Claire came and she got mad,' Kim said darkly. 'She got mad when Gran told her you an' Daddy had gone. She said she wasn't wastin' her time unless Daddy was here, and then Gran got mad, too. I don't like Claire!' he added, with a fierce frown.

They had found a very disgruntled little boy when they returned this afternoon. Not even Sacha could charm him out of behaving badly when he met his grandmother, and later ate his supper, but as Katie got him ready for bed he showed signs of forgiving them, and when she reached for his night light he wanted a kiss.

'Please let me stay up a little longer, Mummy. You're so pretty,' he added coaxingly, and with such an obvious attempt at flattery that she burst out laughing.

'O.K., you win, you little monkey!' She was smiling as she left him. The light would still be burning when she came home tonight from the party, but sometimes it didn't hurt to relax the rules.

She had certainly tried to look pretty tonight, she told herself, for she was aware of just what this party meant. A chance to beat Claire on her own ground; a chance to meet Sacha's friends and, she hoped, impress them that she could be just as attractive, witty and charming as their hostess. A chance to find out for once and for all the truth about how Sacha felt about Claire. And the truth shall make me free, Katie paraphrased cynically.

Was it only yesterday that she had bought this dress? As she glimpsed her reflection in the mirror, she thought that it seemed more like a year ago since she had tried it on in the discreetly luxurious shop and decided then how well it would do for Claire's party.

She had chosen well. The colour was hot pink, and the dress was sheer and swingy around her sandalled feet with a camisole top that left her tanned shoulders and arms bare and clung lovingly to her bosom. With it she wore a matching jacket, its sheerness just enough for the outdoor chill. The whole effect, with Sacha's diamonds and her hair a shining, blonde-streaked mass loose on her shoulders, was designed to make her look expensive, chic and smart— all the adjectives, in other words, that Sacha would automatically expect to have describe a woman he had chosen.

A soft tap at the door brought her head around. For a moment she wondered if it could be Sacha, whose attitude had confused her ever since leaving the house this afternoon. He had stopped half way home and turned to her with a mocking gleam.

'Better do something about that shirt,' he drawled, brushing sawdust from her hair. His hand lingered at her throat. 'You look like you've been thoroughly kissed; we'd better not give Oscar too many clues. His humour can be a little raw at times.'

Katie had flushed scarlet and hurried to obey him, brushing down her shirt and jeans. But since then he had treated her with his usual cool indifference. In fact, the whole episode might not have happened except for an odd gleam when he looked at her, a sort of lazy complacency that had nothing to do with jealousy and might have a great deal to do with possessiveness.

With fast beating heart, she opened the door to her mother-in-law, who was smiling nervously. Marjorie was dazzling in green chiffon with a skilfully draped neckline, and whatever miracle she had worked on her face had taken years off.

'May I come in?'

'Of course.' Katie stepped back.

Marjorie was carrying a large, gaily wrapped box. 'I brought something for Kim,' she said brightly. 'I dug it out of my bag while I was unpacking.'

As though on cue, Kim appeared in the doorway. His thumb was in his mouth and his eyes fixed on the interesting box in his grandmother's hands. He hadn't yet made up his mind about Marjorie, letting his 'wait and see' attitude speak for him, but he was willing to meet her halfway when it came to the matter of presents.

Marjorie smiled at him and Katie caught her breath. It was the same coaxing smile that she had seen on Kim's face five minutes earlier.

'Would you like a present, Kim? May I give it to him, Katie?'

Katie wondered wryly if Marjorie really expected her to say no under the circumstances, but she willingly gave her consent. When the box was opened and the gifts discovered—toy soldiers and a cardboard cut-out Old West Fort—Kim was thrilled, and immediately flung himself on the floor to play with it.

'It's absurd of me, I know, but I'm nervous about going downstairs alone. Would you mind if I went with you?' Marjorie pleaded.

'Of course. Is it because of Sacha?' Katie could sympathise with anyone who was afraid of Sacha.

'Sacha? Oh, no, it's Paul. I'm—a little shy of Paul.'

She was blushing slightly. Katie's eyes widened. She had thought Paul the soul of courtesy today when he met the woman who had left him twenty years ago for another man. Could it be——? Could Marjorie possibly be thinking of a reconciliation? There had been five marriages in between for her, and although Paul might be said to have remained faithful, one could not accuse Marjorie of the same thing.

The flush deepened as though she had guessed what Katie was thinking. 'He's turned into an amazingly attractive man,' she said defensively.

'Wasn't he always?'

'Perhaps he was, but I didn't see it. I was too crazy about Benjamin Thorpe to think of my husband or my son. I suppose I just had to—to grow up a little before I could appreciate what a wonderful man Paul really is.'

'Then it's possible you and Paul may get back together?'

Marjorie looked confused. 'Oh, my dear, it's too early to say what might happen. I'm just glad for the chance to be with him right now, so we can—er—explore our feelings, particularly now that you and Sacha have straightened out your differences.'

Katie saw that her mother-in-law was an incurable romantic and would probably always be searching for the perfect mate. If she was lucky, this time she might convince Paul that she had had a change of heart. And it would really take luck to do that. So far as the other was concerned, what gave Marjorie the idea that she and Sacha had straightened out their differences?

It would soon be time to leave for the party, for they were not having dinner, since Claire was having a *luai*. As Katie accompanied Marjorie downstairs, she wondered how many people would attend. She had submitted a list of twenty names and Sacha probably had more. There might be as many as seventy-five people there—a crowd. Katie wasn't looking forward to it, but a *luai* was informal enough to make conversation easy.

Sacha and Paul were waiting for them and Marjorie fluttered to Paul's side like a gauzy green moth fluttering to a flame. Sacha looked directly at Katie and held out her drink, willing her to join him. He was talking to his grandmother and she crossed the room reluctantly. She saw his eyes lingering on her bruised mouth, still swollen as an aftermath of his kisses. She licked her lips nervously and a gleam, almost of satisfaction, glinted briefly in his eyes before he half closed his lids. Katie found it disturbing, that brief flash of primitive man beneath the civilised veneer of formal cream velvet coat and dark trousers.

'Why are you looking at me like that?' he teased.

'You know why,' she said accusingly. 'You—you hurt me this afternoon, and I believe you're glad.'

'Of course I am.' His voice held an undertone of laughter. 'I enjoyed it. And you can stop looking at me like a wounded doe. You enjoyed it, too, if you'll admit the truth.'

She flushed. 'You—you're unspeakable!' she whispered shakily.

'Beyond the pale,' he agreed solemnly, but his eyes were dancing as they sought hers. 'Come on over here. Gran wants to speak to you.'

Madam Kimberly smiled graciously, as though they might never have quarrelled. 'How beautiful you look tonight, my dear.'

'Thank you, Madam,' Katie said coolly.

'I understand you're going to live on Kauai?'

Katie choked. 'I—yes, I believe so.'

'Good. I'm glad you're remaining in Hawaii. I did not know this, you understand? Claire said you would persuade Sacha to leave the islands,' she added apologetically.

Sacha frowned. 'Claire knows no more about my business than anyone else. Oscar gave me that land years ago, after I expressed a wish to live there some day. I'm sorry if it means leaving you and my father, Gran, but you know I'll see you often.'

She looked at him reflectively, then at Katie. 'Yes. Well, I only want you to be happy.'

Marjorie sighed mournfully. 'Indeed we do. It's almost impossible to achieve—happiness—without love. I don't think I can live without love,' she added theatrically.

A fleeting look of amusement crossed Madam Kimberly's face. 'Indeed? You might do well to remember, Marjorie, that one can't roast a boar over a bed of cold ashes,' she said dryly.

Marjorie gasped indignantly, and Sacha said quickly, 'Aren't you coming to the party, Gran? I thought you wouldn't miss it.'

'No, my dear boy. I'm too old for big parties, and besides, Claire and I came to a mutual understanding today that I would do well to remain at home.'

'Shall we go, then?' Sacha put his glass down abruptly. 'Shall I drive, Father, or you?'

In the resulting confusion, Madam Kimberly rolled up to Katie and touched her hand.

'I mean what I said, Katie. I want you to be happy.'

Claire's home was glittering with lights and they were strung in the trees and along the drive. With the band blaring, the incredible level of noise and people wandering in and out, the house had all the brassy quality of a nightclub. As they pulled up behind a long line of cars, Katie panicked. All these people to meet her! Sacha, opening the door, took one look at her face and took her arm reassuringly.

'I won't know half of them, either,' he muttered.

Claire was apparently waiting for them, for she met them at the foyer door. Her outfit made Katie gasp. Even Marjorie, who was used to the topless bathing suits on the French Riviera, raised her eyebrows. As she had promised, Claire was wearing a jumpsuit, a black one of some shiny material that hugged her svelte figure from the waist down like a second skin. But above the narrow silver belt the black blouse was provocatively sheer, its two strategically placed patch pockets being the only concealment offered for Claire's nakedness.

Fully aware of the stunning impact she made, Claire flaunted them all a defiant smile, then pulled Sacha's head down and kissed him deeply on the mouth. She looked almost drunken with excitement, and there was a hint of desperation about her smile, as though she was risking everything on one throw of the cards tonight in an attempt to either make or break her relationship with Sacha.

He did not exactly repulse her, but he drew away as quickly as possible and at the same time patted her arm gently. Apparently this was enough to encourage Claire, for as she turned to greet Katie her face wore a look of barely concealed malice.

'Hello there,' she purred. 'I was told that you were on Kauai today seeing our house. I feel as though it's mine, too,' she added, with a laughing look at Sacha, 'since I helped with the plans and have been in on the whole thing from the beginning. I was the one who persuaded Sacha to put the studio windows so they face the ocean and the afternoon sun. And isn't the beach deliciously private? I'm looking forward to lying on that beach, sunbathing all over.'

Katie, of course, knew what she was trying to do, but that didn't make it any less painful to hear Claire talking so intimately of the house she hoped to share with Sacha. Her imagination summoned up dozens of pictures of scenes like that one this afternoon, only with Claire and Sacha the participants this time.

A warm, possessive arm slid around her waist and Sacha pulled her to him. 'I don't think Katie was noticing the beach,' he said gravely. 'We got tied up in the house. Er—in one of the bedrooms, as a matter of fact.'

He was looking at her, compelling her to meet his laughing eyes and share their secret. Blushing rosily, Katie darted a quick look at him, then away. Anyone, seeing her face, knew exactly what had happened today.

Claire drew in a sharp, hissing breath, her face whitening with pain and fury. She looked blindly over their heads, then saw Marjorie.

'Darling!' she gushed, leaning forward and touching her cheek. 'How lovely you look! You simply must give me the name of your plastic surgeon. An old friend—of my mother's, actually—is looking for one, and I'm sure you can recommend yours.'

It was a crude, unprovoked attack, and wouldn't have been made if Claire hadn't been slightly off balance with anger. But Marjorie was equal to it.

'Precious,' she cooed, 'I'll be glad to. But are you sure it's for a friend? I thought perhaps when you dressed tonight, you realised you needed something—er—lifted.' Her eyes dropped significantly to Claire's breasts, clearly outlined beneath the sheer blouse. 'It's sad but true that one needs a superb figure to go naked.'

Claire's mouth tightened with temper, but she made a valiant recovery. 'Which should prevent you from ever trying it, *darling*,' she said sweetly. 'Please go on inside. You'll find food, drinks, dancing. There's even a little grass smoking by some of Katie's friends.'

They were soon separated from Sacha's parents by the crush of the crowd. They found the largest group in the big playroom at the back of the house, where the band had been set up. The air was throbbing with the rhythm of steel guitars and a long line of hula girls in grass skirts was weaving through the dancing couples. On the fringe were little knots of people huddled together, screaming in an attempt to make conversation. The whole scene was madly disorganised and the noise level was penetrating. Sacha looked around disgustedly and his mouth moved. Katie could only guess at his words, but when he plunged into the dancing couples she flung herself after him.

He led her through the nearest doorway and into another room, where the quietness was like a benediction. Here most of Katie's friends had gathered, sitting around talking. One of the young men had a guitar, and he was sitting crosslegged on the floor, strumming it with muted notes. These were the people Claire had accused of smoking grass, but the cigarettes Katie saw were not grass, and the drinking was confined to a few glasses of wine. They were mostly artists—the people who had supplied the crafts and art work for her shop—and they obviously felt out of place here, and had gathered in one room to enjoy themselves.

'Hi there, hon!'

It was Pat. She was talking to a bearded young man and her ex-husband, Chuck, who was something of a ladies' man, was nearby, talking animatedly to a girl in a calico skirt and peasant blouse.

Everyone looked up at Pat's greeting and hailed Katie delightedly. Sacha was introduced and soon absorbed into the group, for they all knew of his talent and respected it. Room was made for Katie on one of the sofas and Sacha sat on the floor, leaning his head against her knee. From the relaxed away he joined in the conversation, she knew that he was enjoying himself.

Finally Pat joined her, huddling on the floor beside Sacha.

'Having a good time?' she whispered.

'I am now,' Katie smiled. 'What do you think of this place?'

'So far, fabulous! I haven't been all over the house yet, but I couldn't see it, anyway. The crowd's too big. Have you been outside yet?' Pat added.

'No, we just got here.'

'There's a *luai* and the food is delicious. Chuck and I stuffed ourselves, but we were feeling kinda lost in that crowd of millionaires, so we sort of drifted in here. Can you believe it, Katie? Claire charted a *jet* to bring over her guests from Honolulu! It was one big party all the way. Drinks flowing, hors d'oeuvres, the whole bit. Now, I know how the rich live!'

Katie frowned. 'Not all the time, I assure you,' she said dryly.

'What do you think of Claire's jumpsuit?' Pat lowered her voice. 'She did buy it from Martelle's, just as I told you. But how does she have the nerve to wear something like that in public? Everyone's talking about her! What's she trying to prove, anyhow? That her figure is good? We knew that already!'

Sacha moved abruptly. 'Come on, Katie, let's get some food.'

She followed him out meekly. She knew he was leaving because he had overhead Pat's remarks. What did he expect? she thought resentfully. It was the truth. Did he think he could keep people from talking?

The passageway they were in opened on to the lawn. Here, the bar and *luai* had been set up on tables and there were a vast number of white-coated waiters to handle the crowd. And more hula girls. The lawn was landscaped in a series of tiers, and the bottom tier contained the big swimming pool, complete with cabañas, loungers and tables. The underwater lights were on, outlining its cloverleaf shape in luminous blue. The crowd was dispersed all over the lawn, which was blazing with lights. Looking around bewilderedly, Katie wondered if half the population of the islands was present. All these people to meet her? It was ludicrous.

'First order of business. Would you like some food or a drink?' Sacha's grim face was unsmiling.

Katie felt a twinge of guilt. Loving Claire as he did, Pat's words must have hurt. 'Sacha, I'm sorry. Pat had no right to talk about Claire that way. She——'

'Save it, Katie,' he interrupted curtly. 'I don't want to listen to it, if you please. Claire's none of Pat's business, nor yours, either, so far as that goes. Now,' he added deliberately, 'I asked you what you wanted—a drink or some food? I'll go on my own and battle the *luai* table if you like. I see Julian Fine over there. I'll ask him to wait here with you.'

Katie was burning with resentment. She had been put in her place with a resounding thump and coming after his earlier championship, it hurt. Right now she didn't care what Sacha did, nor how he was hurt. He could go and jump in that elaborate swimming pool for all she cared, she thought viciously. 'Food, if you please,' she said tightly. 'But you needn't bother——'

Once again Sacha anticipated her. 'No bother,' he replied crisply. 'I'm hungry, too. Julian, how about being a good chap and looking after my wife while I get her some food? We're both starving.'

'With pleasure,' Julian said promptly. He glanced at Katie's empty hands. 'Shall I get you something to drink? What will you have?'

Not wanting to take out her bad temper on Julian, Katie made an effort to answer pleasantly. 'Something cold and non-alcoholic, but please, I'd rather you wouldn't——'

'I'll only be a minute. And here's Mr Thorpe, so you won't be alone. Ah, sir, do you know Sacha's wife?'

'Very well. How are you, Katie?'

And, with a sinking feeling of resignation, Katie turned to meet Ben's eyes, dancing with devilry, a-gleam with that small boy look of guilt that knew he shouldn't be doing it, yet was unable to resist the temptation to stir up a little mischief.

'Katie, my sweet, I thought Sacha would never leave,' Ben murmured, as soon as Julian left them. 'I must talk to you. Where can we go to be alone?'

His voice was husky with that mixture of suppressed passion and reproach that was supposed to make a girl feel excited and guilty at the same time, but Katie had his measure by now. The perennial adolescent, like Marjorie, he was always searching for the perfect mate. Oh, Ben was a charming rascal and Katie was even fond of him, but she had no intention of allowing him to destroy her marriage merely in order to indulge his weakness for pursuing beautiful women.

'What nonsense! You know Sacha wouldn't allow it!' she said lightly.

'And you know what I think of *that*!' he replied roughly. His eyes darkened as they roved her face with practised skill. 'Very well, if not tonight, what about tomorrow? Same place as before, same time?'

'No, Ben, I won't let you smash up my marriage.'

'I think it's my *duty* to show you the truth about yourself—and your marriage,' he said righteously. 'I'll wait for you tomorrow.'

Just then she saw him stiffen and looked around to see Sacha approaching them with a purposeful stride. She felt a twinge of fear as she met his dark, glittering eyes.

'Why in hell are you hanging around my wife, Ben? Aren't you a little too old for her?' Sacha's savage contempt must have flicked Ben on the raw, because he flushed with anger.

Katie spoke up hastily, in an attempt to avert disaster. 'Sacha, I'm perfectly capable——'

'You're not capable of a damned thing except the inability to say "no" to this ageing Romeo here!' She felt a humiliated surge of anger as his contempt spilled over on her. 'You stupid little nitwit, he's just trying to get back at me through you. He has a notion it would be fun to add another Kimberly woman to his growing list. Well, Ben?' Sacha turned back to the older man. The passion that thickened his voice was so primitive that it only needed a word, a look, to explode into violence. 'Do you want to take me on? I should warn you I'm not as civilised as my father. I fight dirty—just like you.'

Ben's eyes gleamed. 'Do you really care enough about her to fight for her, Sacha?' he queried sardonically.

Sacha's voice lowered to a growl. 'What's mine, I keep. I've already demonstrated that to you with *Dreaming*.'

Katie stood by, helpless to stop the quarrel that was developing, furious with Sacha for ignoring her explanation, and thankful that, so far, they had not attracted attention. She was not so stupid, despite what Sacha said, as to imagine that Sacha cared enough to fight for her. No, this quarrel had its roots in past years, in Claire.

'What's going on?' Claire's light, amused voice broke up the tension. Suddenly both men seemed to realise where they were. 'You two look like you're ready to enter the ring for the championship boxing match! Can it be? Oh, no, let me guess,' she added coyly. 'Is it possible that Daddy is staking a claim at last, and you feel obliged to object, darling, because she's your wife?' Her clear, tinkling voice held an undertone of malice. 'If so, don't waste your time. Daddy has already taken over your little mouse. It's too late now for you to make noises like an outraged husband.'

Sacha looked at her impassively. 'Claire, shut up.'

She flinched and a hint of red appeared on the dusky cheekbones. 'B-b-but, Sacha, I'm just trying to keep you from making a fool of yourself by chasing after a woman who's already cut you out of her life! Be thankful for it. She's not worth your time, anyway.'

Sacha looked at Ben, who was watching Claire with an oddly curious look on his face. 'For God's sake, Ben,' Sacha said wearily, 'can't you do something about her? I've wet-nursed your daughter for years, trying to repair the damage that your neglect has done. Pampering her bruised little ego, seeing her through teenage crushes and aborted love affairs, even a smashed marriage. But after tonight I'm through. It's your turn, Ben. Can't you forget your damned womanising long enough to clean up your own back yard? For instance, what in the hell were you about when you let her wear that outfit tonight?'

Claire looked stupefied. It must have been the first time in her spoiled, self-indulgent life that she saw herself as others saw her. She would have thoroughly enjoyed a fight with Katie, but for Sacha to criticise her was a shocking revelation. Her beauty disappeared so suddenly that it was frightening, and she looked like a predatory animal about to strike as she hissed, 'How dare you? I wore it because of *you*! You—you painted her.' Her eyes, black with fury, moved stiffly to Katie. 'You said I didn't make a good subject. I wanted you to see that I could—that I was—th-that my portrait could be as famous as *Dreaming*! I did it for you,' she added, on a wailing note.

'See what I mean?' Sacha asked Ben tiredly.

'My God! Claire, my child, take hold of yourself,' Ben said compassionately.

'Come on, Katie, let's get out of here,' Sacha said bitterly.

They passed Julian, who, with a drink in either hand,

stared after them wonderingly. Sacha had to pause several times to acknowledge greetings from people who knew him, but he was short to the point of curtness and he did not stop to talk until they reached the car.

'What about your parents?' Katie asked, as he held the door open for her.

'Leave them. They'll get a ride with someone, and if they don't, Ben will send them home in one of his cars. Don't make waves, Katie,' he added tautly. 'I want to get home. We have a lot of things to get out of the way that I've been putting off far too long.'

At the entrance to the small living room, where the family usually met before dinner, Sacha stopped her. She followed him reluctantly as he pulled her into the room and closed the door, trapping them within its cosy intimacy.

'Please, not tonight, Sacha.' Her eyes were dark with torment. 'I know you're tired and heartsick, but so am I. Just remember that things will be much brighter in the morning.'

'What the hell is that supposed to mean?' he asked harshly.

'Claire,' she explained shakily. 'Claire will be ashamed and sorry tomorrow, and everything will be back to the way it was before when you forgive her.'

She cried out as he took a swift step forward, his eyes flaring with anger. Uttering a curse through tightly clenched teeth, he reached for her and gripping her forearms, pulled her against the lean, hard, arrogant lines of his body.

'Will it?' he asked sarcastically. 'Will everything be the same tomorrow, my sweet wife?'

She was frightened, but she did not waver. 'Yes.' She met his eyes bravely. 'You can't change how you feel over-night—I know that. You've always loved Claire and you're not about to change merely because she has temporarily disillusioned you. I just don't like being used as a convenience while you wait to make up your quarrel with her!' she added, a shade defiantly.

'It looks like there's only one way to shut you up,' he said coldly.

Katie fought desperately to stop him from taking her lips, pushing and beating frantically at his shoulders, but her efforts were puny. He was too strong and cruel for her to withstand the insistent pressure of his arms. Sobbing beneath her breath, she turned her head from side to side, shivering at the feel of his cool mouth sliding over her soft skin. At last he captured his desperately evading quarry, and once that predatory mouth met hers, Katie knew herself lost. With a groan she surrendered her lips, her mouth parting beneath the intensity of his fiercely possessive kiss. Shamelessly she clung to him, long shudders rippling her body as she gave herself up to the drugging sweetness of his kiss. Finally he raised his head, long enough to mutter her name against her mouth, and with a soft moan of protest she encircled his neck and pressed her soft body against his. Sacha drew a sharp breath, then slid a warm hand beneath her chin and tilted it to meet his triumphant eyes.

'This is one way we've always been able to communicate, isn't it, Katie?' he asked unsteadily.

She nodded dumbly, too drained of resistance to summon up even a flash of her former defiance.

'Is this my Katie?' he teased. 'No fight left? Does this mean you give up? Throw in the towel? Admit you're mine?'

She sighed, her blue-veined lids closing over eyes that sought to mask their shamed hunger from his probing search.

'Katie?' His voice was whisper-soft. 'I'm waiting for your surrender.'

His lips captured hers again, but this time his kiss was slower, easier, its warm sensuality carrying her along on the full tide of his passion as he frankly demanded the totality of her submission. He withdrew his lips and ran them softly over the closed, quivering eyelids.

'You win, Sacha,' she murmured huskily. 'I love you. Please don't put me out of your life. I want to live with you on any terms. I'll even share you with Claire if I have to.'

She slid her arms convulsively around his neck and, standing on tiptoe, pressed hot kisses on the strong brown column of his throat. He had stiffened at her confession, and for a brief, humiliating moment she thought he was going to throw it back in her face. Then, his voice husky and tender, he bent over her and lifted her into his arms. 'Katie—dear heart! I'm over-whelmed with shame! Is that what you believe? I said we had to have a talk, and I'm just beginning to realise how much.'

He carried her to one of the deep, plump armchairs and sat down with her in his lap.

'My sweet, I've been cruel and hurt you. Will you forgive me?'

Tempting as it was to give herself up to the seductive bliss of lying in his arms, Katie knew that she could not afford to do so, so she struggled upright. Darting him a quick look, she replied uncertainly, 'I suppose I was sort of unreasonable at times myself.'

Sacha smiled and ran a finger down her flushed cheek, making her pulses leap.

'Not unreasonable—no. You had a right to my trust and I didn't give it. I just wish you'd told me why you didn't want me to go to my grandmother that night. Why didn't you tell me about the pressures she and Claire were putting on you?' he asked curiously.

'I didn't think you'd believe me,' she said humbly.

His mouth tightened. 'No, I guess I hadn't given you any reason to think I would, had I?'

'Wh-who told you?'

'Pat. And later, Gran confessed to what she'd done.' A slight smile flickered on his lips. 'I was very angry that afternoon in Honolulu. Angry and fed up. I had reason to hate and fear Ben Thorpe and it looked as if you were falling for his line, behaving like the child I thought you were. I was breathing fire when I got to the shop, and Pat turned on me like a small virago. Within five minutes, she'd taken me apart, and in the process revealed more about how you felt and what you thought then I'd got from you in the six years of our marriage. I was stunned to hear that instead of hating the idea of this reconciliation, as I had thought, you loved me. I was also shocked to hear what Gran and Claire had said to you and what you thought I felt about you. It was so totally untrue, darling. Oh, I'd known Gran was very pro-Claire, but she knew how I really felt. And it didn't occur to me that you would listen to Claire when I'd made it clear that I wanted you back as my wife.'

'Claire said it all depended on Kim,' Katie tried to explain. 'And she was right. Kim *was* the reason you wanted me back. You said so.'

Sacha turned her head gently to his. 'Katie, I love our son, naturally, but surely you know that I love you even more? Not want you! I was just thankful that Kim gave me an excuse to force you back into my arms.' He groaned softly. 'You little idiot, why do you think I married you?'

'Because you wanted me, and also felt responsible for me.'

'Yes, I'm sure that was the impression Irene West fostered in you,' he said wryly.

'But wasn't it true, Sacha? And you said that you needed

a mother for Kim——'

'I said a lot of damn fool things in an attempt not to scare you to death about this reconciliation!' he interrupted savagely. 'I admit I didn't really understand my motives for marrying you, but it wasn't long before I saw that you were just what I wanted. But you were jealous and insecure. I put it down to your age and kept hoping it would change, that you might have a baby and that would help. But the night I left for New York, when we quarrelled, I decided that a divorce was the only answer. Later, when I learned from Irene West of the pressure she'd been putting on you, I knew it wasn't altogether your fault, but I hoped that a few days of thinking about a divorce might work wonders. I came home expecting to find you properly humbled, and ready to fall into my arms. You can imagine my shock when I found you'd gone. I nearly went crazy. I searched for you everywhere, and finally had to give up. After that, I finished *Dreaming* and put it in the contest hoping to flush you out of hiding. When it didn't, I pulled up stakes and spent a year with Oscar and Ellie, painting, little knowing that you were on the next island, struggling to make ends meet with a baby and a shop.'

'I didn't know you'd want to hear from me,' Katie confessed miserably. 'I sometimes thought of letting you know where I was, but I thought you might be embarrassed to hear from me.'

'Embarrassed? God, no!' he groaned. His warm breath stirred the hair at her temples. 'How could you think that? Well, easily enough, I suppose. I hadn't given you reason to think anything else.' His firm mouth trembled slightly and for the first time since she had known him his face was naked and totally vulnerable to pain. 'Even after I learned what had been happening to you, you made me so damned jealous about Ben that I was brutal. It wasn't until we got home, and I saw your reaction to the kidnapping and learned from Gran what she'd done, that I began to see what we Kimberlys had put you through. Gran's sorry now, Katie, but she almost destroyed us, didn't she?'

'I thought I'd wait and see how you felt.' Her voice gave away very little of the agonies she had been through. 'But it did seem to be Claire, all the way.'

'I could kill her! She was jealous of you, of course, because she always had my attention, and she couldn't stand to give it up. But, Katie, you've got to believe me—there was never anything between us. *Never*. She was like a sister, a spoiled, demanding sister. I've seen her through everything from measles to a smashed-up marriage, and when it blew up in her face, I encouraged her to buy the ranch next to us because we're the only family she's ever had.'

'But she left her husband because of you.'

'Is that what she told you?' A lingering trace of gall remained in his smile. 'He threw her out, but I had nothing to do with it, I assure you.'

'But everyone said—even Ben——'

'Everyone was wrong, including Ben,' Sacha said bleakly. 'He had his own reasons for thinking that—and telling it to you. But Tony Wetherell threw her out—and I wasn't the "other man" involved. Oh, I knew she hinted that I was the cause of the break-up, and I let it slide rather than make a fool out of her by denying it. It saved her pride and didn't seem to harm me. But I never dreamed she'd try to peddle that story to *you*!' His mouth twisted.

He sounded so cross and irritable that Katie put her arms around his neck and kissed his mouth. It was the first time she had ever had the opportunity to feel superior to her husband, so she felt like making the most of it. Really, she thought amusedly, Sacha had been rather naïve about Claire. Another woman would have had her measure a long time ago.

'Hmmm, nice,' he breathed, gathering her closely into his arms.

'No.' She planted her palms firmly on his shoulders and held him away from her. 'Not until I've had a few more explanations, if you please. Sacha! I'm serious,' she added breathlessly.

'Oh, very well.' He released her reluctantly. 'What do you want to know?'

'Why were you so upset and angry tonight about—well, about the way people were talking about Claire, if you really don't love her?'

'My anger was with Claire, not with other people,' he said quietly. 'I recognised that she was making a final attempt to hold on to what she had, and that she was headed for a breakdown if she didn't get her own way. I knew Ben. He'd probably expect me to assume the responsibility for her, as usual. By then I'd learned that she'd systematically worked to undermine our marriage, and I wasn't having any more of it. You see,' he added seriously, 'Claire knew what that trip to Kauai meant, even if you didn't. It meant that I was pulling out, leaving her, washing my hands of the whole sickening mess at last. She never had been my responsibility, really, except that I'd known since I was a boy how neglected she was, and felt sorry for her.'

'And I had to complicate things for you by being so jealous!' Katie mourned.

'Don't apologise.' Sacha grinned. 'That jealousy was just about my only comfort when I thought you didn't care anything about me. When I finally cut through all the hostility and non-communication, and learned what was going on, I was determined to get you to Kauai, kicking and screaming, if necessary,' the grin widened, 'and present you with the accomplished fact of a home. I knew you were trying to back paddle your little canoe as fast as you could, but I didn't intend to let you get away with it this time. I thought I'd lead up to it nice and easy, but then you gave me that prissy little speech, and all hell broke loose.' He reached out and stroked the outline of her mouth with caressing fingertips. 'Not that I'm at all sorry. It was the most satisfying half hour of my life, and personally, I haven't regretted a moment of it. No matter how many times we make love in that bedroom, I'll never forget the first time.'

'What will happen to Claire now?' she asked, when her blushes had begun to subside. 'Will sh-she continue to live here?'

He recognised the fearful note in her voice, and said reassuringly, 'I don't think so. Ben isn't Chairman of the Board of a dozen companies for nothing. He has a great gift for organisation. Now that he recognises the problem, he'll deal with it, very efficiently, very correctly, and the first thing he'll do is take Claire away from here. Who knows? The whole thing may be the making of him.'

She looked up warily. 'You were angry with Ben tonight.'

The dark flash in his eyes was savage. 'I could have killed him!' he said thickly. 'When he laid his hand on your arm, I wanted to break it in two. I've never felt that way about anyone before. You're mine, Katie, and I'm not going to let anyone take you away.' He buried his face in her throat, pressing his lips against the fluttering pulse at its base.

Her hands tangled in the black hair, and she ran her hands through it tenderly before cupping the hard, arrogant face between her palms. 'Love me, darling,' she begged achingly. 'Love me now.'

'Everyone loves romance at Christmas'

The Mills & Boon Christmas Gift Pack is available from October 9th in the U.K. It contains four new paperback Romances from four favourite authors, in an attractive presentation case:

The Silken Cage	– Rebecca Stratton
Egyptian Honeymoon	– Elizabeth Ashton
Dangerous	– Charlotte Lamb
Freedom to Love	– Carole Mortimer

You do not pay any extra for the pack – so put it on your Christmas shopping list now.
On sale where you buy paperbacks, £3.00 (U.K. net).

The rose of romance
Mills & Boon

Mills & Boon
Best Seller Romances

The very best of Mills & Boon Romances
brought back for those of you who missed
them when they were first published.
In October
we bring back the following four
great romantic titles.

THE AUTOCRAT OF MELHURST
by Anne Hampson

Claire had promised Simon Condliffe that she would stay on
in her job as nanny to his small niece as long as he needed her
— but she hadn't bargained on falling in love with him, and
then having to watch him with his close friend — or was she
his fiancée? — Ursula Corwell.

LORD OF ZARACUS
by Anne Mather

When Carolyn joined her archaeologist father in Mexico, she
found herself immediately in conflict with Don Carlos, who
owned the valley where her father was searching for a Zapotec
city. Don Carlos thought she was 'a typical product of the
permissive society' and Carolyn let him know that 'I am not
one of your peons'. It seemed an inauspicious beginning to
their relationship. And yet—

LOGAN'S ISLAND
by Mary Wibberley

Helen had inherited an island off the coast of Brazil — jointly
with an unknown man called Jake Logan. Its name — Island
of Storms — just about summed up the wildly antagonistic
relationship that promptly developed between the two of
them!

LOVE'S PRISONER
by Violet Winspear

Meeting Lafe Sheridan proved a milestone in Eden's young
life, and she knew that no man would ever mean as much to
her. But her beautiful sister had more effect on him . . . He
was rich and lonely, and Gale had always meant to marry a
rich man . . .

If you have difficulty in obtaining any of these books through
your local paperback retailer, write to:

Mills & Boon Reader Service
P.O. Box 236, Thornton Road, Croydon, Surrey, CR9 3RU.